Praise for Charlie Cochrane's
Lessons in Temptation

"I think I'm going to have to either go round to Charlie Cochrane's house and stop her from writing anything else, or stop reviewing her books on the site because it's becoming embarrassing as to how much we all like them."

~ *Speak Its Name*

"Charlie's trademark dialog and humor come through, making it a joy to read..."

~ *Reviews by Jessewave*

"The characters really drive this story and their interactions and dialogue illuminate their personalities perfectly."

~ *The Romance Studio*

Look for these titles by *Charlie Cochrane*

Now Available:

Cambridge Fellows Mysteries
Lessons in Love
Lessons in Desire
Lessons in Discovery
Lessons in Power
Lessons in Temptation
Lessons in Seduction
Lessons in Trust

Lessons
in Temptation

A Cambridge Fellows Mystery

Charlie Cochrane

A Samhain Publishing, Ltd. publication.

Samhain Publishing, Ltd.
577 Mulberry Street, Suite 1520
Macon, GA 31201
www.samhainpublishing.com

Lessons in Temptation
Copyright © 2010 by Charlie Cochrane
Print ISBN: 978-1-60504-862-8
Digital ISBN: 978-1-60504-845-1

Cover by Scott Carpenter

First Samhain Publishing, Ltd. electronic publication: December 2009
First Samhain Publishing, Ltd. print publication: October 2010

Dedication

For my family and friends, especially the ones who put up with inane questions about whether parts of a plot will work. And for my editor, Deborah, because she hasn't strangled me. Yet.

Chapter One

"Now, for goodness sake promise me that you'll behave yourselves while you're down in Bath. I know people there..." Jonty's mother's words still rang in his ears. He and Orlando had broken their journey from Cambridge at the Stewarts's London home, where they'd been treated like undernourished, miscreant seven year olds, not like strapping, highly respected Cambridge college lecturers.

Jonty took a sidelong, affectionate glance at the man walking beside him. Orlando Coppersmith—his lover, colleague, soul mate, and by turns the most annoying and the most wonderful creature in the universe.

"I can see why people want to live here." Orlando gestured towards the city, which shone in the July sunshine, nestling snugly below the hill. They were walking along the towpath of the canal and the mellow Bath Stone all around looked like honey and cream. Or the ice cream with which they were stuffing their faces.

"It looks lovely now, I'll grant you, although this sort of masonry can seem very drab when it's raining. That's when you need to see a place, Dr. Coppersmith, when it's wet and grey, then you'll know if you want to live there. I remember going to the New Forest when I was a boy and thinking it was absolute heaven. When we went back in February a more bleak and ghastly hole I'd never seen—it put me right off the area."

"I'll take your word for the New Forest. Certainly part of the appeal of both Cambridge and the Old Manor is they're as delightful in fog or storm as in the height of summer."

Jonty smiled at the urbanity his friend displayed; the old Orlando wouldn't have been so worldly wise. He wasn't the same person he'd been in November 1905 when they first met and it was a remarkable transformation. "Galatea."

"I beg your pardon?"

"Sorry, I was thinking aloud. You being Galatea to my Pygmalion, and all that."

Orlando snorted. "So you took the rough stone and made a wonderful creature? Thank you for the compliment."

"Daft beggar. I didn't mean you started off rough—you've always been well spoken and your manners are beautiful, it's just..." He didn't need to add "you were like a child in how you understood the world." They both knew that.

"I suppose I've grown up a lot, these last two years." Orlando's naturally stern face lit up into a smile which emphasised just how handsome he could be when he tried. Dark, slim, elegant, a total contrast to the blond ball of muscle, half a head shorter, at his side.

They'd arrived in Bath the day before and taken a suite at the Grand Hotel for a couple of weeks. Orlando needed to view some mathematical incunabula which his department might want to acquire, and his *other half* had insisted on coming too, bringing a manuscript which he needed to work on. The university had a month's grace to decide whether they wished to purchase any or all of the mathematical books and Orlando anticipated that he'd only want a week to inspect them, so that time could be spread out, interspersed with some sightseeing and touring. Or wandering along waterways indulging themselves.

"So what did you get up to this morning?" Orlando wiped the last drips of ice cream from his fingers.

"I'm not sure, but the time whizzed past." Jonty grimaced, vainly trying to get his own hands clean, his handkerchief fighting a losing battle. "I formulated what will turn out to be a brilliant first paragraph for my book, located a number of decent restaurants and I found the cricket club." He counted them off on his sticky fingers. "Ooh and I even tracked down somewhere we can take the therapeutic waters should you wish to do so."

"You did better than me, then." Orlando took a long, discontented sniff. "I've underestimated the amount of work involved in assessing all these manuscripts—you should see how decrepit they are. When I look at those piles of books, for the first time in my life I wish I could swap university work for a bit of detecting."

They walked in silence for a while. "There's not been a lot of that over the last few months, has there?" The question didn't need an answer. Late spring and early summer had been pleasant enough—dunderheads and tripos, May bumps and punting on the river, roses blooming in their garden— Cambridge at her loveliest and life at its mellowest. Jonty had loved every moment, revelling in the respite and recuperation it allowed. Orlando hadn't been as happy.

"Don't think I'm not content, Dr. Stewart." Orlando gently touched Jonty's arm. "I'm as satisfied as any man could be in our house." He lowered his voice to a whisper. "With you at my side and a double bed to share every night, but..."

"But you miss a bit of murder and mayhem." Jonty clapped his lover's shoulder. "I've known that, even if you haven't said.

11

You've become accustomed to having a mystery to apply your brain to on a regular basis and now there's not even a sniff of a corpse on the horizon."

There'd been a couple of little mysteries brought to their attention, although they were trivial and one of them had irked Orlando considerably. He was a man who was used to being consulted by detective inspectors, commissioned by the college master to solve problems that had remained unexplained for many years, and now the only commissions he seemed to be getting were banal.

"Can you blame me? I hardly think an accusation of plagiarism at St. Francis's College is meat enough to chew on."

"Not beneath your dignity, though. Not like Miss Peters's undergarments." Jonty could barely restrain his giggles.

"I can't believe we were consulted, for heaven's sake, on the matter of who was stealing small clothes off someone's washing line." Orlando rolled his eyes, looking like a Shakespearian heroine.

"Not just 'someone'. The sister of the Master of St. Bride's. Our college's honour was at stake." Jonty poked his lover's ribs. "And you're just cross because I solved it and you didn't."

"I don't know what you mean." The blush which crept up Orlando's cheek was fetching. "And why women should have so many frills and ribbons incorporated into an item that wouldn't be in public view staggers me. Weren't you shocked?"

"When we saw exhibit A? No. I helped put together my sister Lavinia's trousseau, so none of it was a shock. And don't think you can change the subject. I'm sure you were eagerly anticipating working out the mystery by intellect alone, only to find that I'd flushed out the culprits." Jonty still savoured the rare taste of triumph over his friend.

"I wouldn't mind if you'd used that sawdust which your

dear mama calls brains, but you did it by sheer prosaic observation."

"I think it was a stroke of genius, taking to the shrubbery in the kitchen garden of the Lodge. I suppose the fact that the perpetrators turned out to be from our old enemy, the college next door, is no consolation?" Jonty knew it wasn't; Orlando was taking this hard.

"It might have proved so, if it hadn't been for your father." Orlando's ears almost had steam coming out of them.

"Ah. I wondered when that would get a mention." Richard Stewart had been consulted in May—by King Edward himself, no less—to look into the matter of some missing letters. "The pair of them are old friends, Dr. Coppersmith."

Orlando didn't answer for a while. When he spoke at last, his voice was like a little boy's. "I just feel it was the sort of thing *we* should have been consulted upon. Now we're miles away from home and even if a bit of mischief happens, the local police are hardly likely to be calling us in, unless by some ridiculous coincidence Inspector Wilson happens to be here too."

"I wouldn't be hoping for that, either." A nasty little frisson went down Jonty's back. "If a murder does occur in our immediate vicinity these two weeks, any policeman would immediately suspect *us*. As Inspector Wilson keeps pointing out, we have an annoying habit of being too close to sudden death."

"Hm. You could be right." Orlando's voice was grudging. "It just makes me feel such a failure."

"For goodness sake, haven't we got plenty to keep us occupied? A fortnight here and then a proper holiday. A nice long train journey across to the south of France, days on end exploring the delights of Monaco and Nice." Jonty screwed up

13

his eyes, trying to superimpose the image of the Riviera on the mellow Bath Stone. "It'll be a glorious month or so."

They wandered back to the Grand, where Jonty wrote up his ideas and Orlando prepared a plan of campaign to tackle most efficiently the acres of volumes he'd have to plough through. This included purchasing some powerful magnifying glasses, as some of the stuff was handwritten, so small that the author might have been a mouse—Orlando would need to study it closely to see if it were a work of genius or just plain dross. The horrific thought that he might have to invest in a pair of spectacles like his lover's was swiftly put to the back of his brain.

Not even the fact that Orlando ended the evening by saying he needed "an early night, not an 'early night', Jonty. I have work in the morning and need all my wits about me," could spoil the day. They were both sure this was going to be an excellent break.

📖

Tuesday dawned overcast, which filled Orlando with joy, given that he'd be spending all the morning cooped up in a stuffy room and much of the afternoon searching for the right kind of magnifying glass. Jonty would be off pursuing things of his own and at least in this weather he couldn't be sunning himself in the gardens of the hotel or finding a rowing boat to scull up the river. Whatever he decided to do was of little consequence so long as he wasn't getting into mischief.

"I'd actually intended to go in search of follies and fantasies." Jonty twitched the knot of his tie into place. "I've a yearning to see the work of Ralph Allen, and the strange long garden at Beckford's old house. They say it stretches for a mile out to the man's monument. I'm sorry, am I boring you?"

"No." Orlando hastily stifled a yawn.

"Liar. Anyway, they'll help to clear my mind. I've a last knotty problem concerning one of the sonnets to sort out for my book." He grinned, made a pantomime bow, then kissed his lover's head, indicating what a good mood he was in. "And the Crescent would leave you cold so I want to admire it without a threnody of discomfort attending me and ruining my pleasure. Right, I'm off. Meet me at Pulteney Bridge, one o'clock sharp, for lunch."

One o'clock had come and long gone by the time Jonty arrived at the restaurant. "You were supposed to be here an hour ago. Where were you?" Orlando bridled. He'd ordered food already, confident that the normally punctual Jonty would be there at exactly the time specified. Luckily he'd only ordered a salad which could sit on the plate awaiting its rightful consumer, although it was looking a bit wilted and rather sad by the time the man arrived.

"Oh, Dr. Coppersmith, I'm sorry. I took a walk up to Ralph Allen's Sham castle—you know, that thing I pointed out yesterday which looks glorious from a distance and close up is more like a theatre set. Well, lo and behold, that's exactly what they're using it for. Lots of activity was going on, so I had to poke my nose in and they're putting on *Macbeth* as an open-air production. The chap I talked to was very keen on authenticity, insisted that they'd be in the plaid and using as close to a real *claidheamh mòr* as they could get. It'll be quite stunning in that location, high above the city—we must get tickets." Jonty's face shone with pleasure.

If Orlando hadn't known it was impossible he would have said that light actually radiated from his friend's very being, as he blethered on about the other great love of his life, one for which Orlando only felt the occasional pang of jealousy.

"Is it a good play then?" He was prepared on this occasion to forgive Jonty the terrible social gaffe he'd committed, punctuality being paramount and all that. He knew how distracted his lover got at any encounter with the Bard, how it could make him go off on all sorts of unexpected tangents. And he loved to see him so happy, particularly as it meant a potential source of amusement for when Orlando was going to be occupied.

"Good? Of course it is. Such a powerful play. The acting won't be as high-quality as that we saw in London for *Hamlet*, of course, but they're said to have a few top-notch people lined up for the main roles and I believe that Lady M. is going to be played in the Elizabethan fashion." His eyes lit up at the thought.

"I don't quite follow…"

"By a man or a boy. Imagine that."

Orlando did and it wasn't pleasant. It may have been good enough for William Shakespeare, but *he* didn't approve. "And you, I presume, are determined to see it?"

"Of course I am. More than that, I've offered to go and help them with some of their production stuff. Getting the props entirely right and doing a bit on the interpretation-of-the-Bard side."

"You volunteered, I imagine?"

"Well, I let slip that I was interested in William S. and the conversation turned to what I did for a living, then they asked if I was free and…"

Orlando didn't need to ask any more. No doubt the Stewart name had been subtly dropped somewhere or other and Jonty had played on both the noble connections and his position at St. Bride's. With a wistful smile, a twinkle of the blue eyes and lots of self-deprecation, naturally. *One of the lesser lights at the university, of course. No great expert, suspect Papa got me my fellowship.* Orlando had seen Jonty's charm in action and potent stuff it was. It always worked on him, for a start.

"It's actually a good idea. It'll keep you out of mischief for a while. I dread to think what you'll get up to if I let you get bored." Orlando grinned indulgently. Sometimes Jonty was just like a little boy, a trait that made his lover even more besotted with him.

"Perhaps they'll even let me play a small part. I could wear the plaid or some fierce rustic outfit. I could even be one of the trees in Birnham Wood!" Jonty took a draught of beer and smiled exultantly. He set to on his salad with his usual startling appetite, oblivious to the fact that it was past its best. A man in training for the theatre needed his sustenance.

"I'll definitely come and see it if you're a tree. In fact, if they give you any part that means you can't speak for two hours that would be an absolute bonus. Should have thought of that strategy ages ago. Ow!" Orlando bent down and rubbed his shin.

"Anyway, I am truly sorry to be late, Dr. Coppersmith. As penance I won't demand that we go around the Abbey this afternoon, although I would like to see it sometime. And with you in tow as you're good with the Latin translations and I'm hopeless. Perhaps we could walk over to the Botanical Gardens instead?"

"So you can see which tree you can wear on your head for this play?"

"That's an excellent idea. Then I can also see which branch I can cut off and apply to your bare backside, I think. You're getting too cheeky for words. I'll have to tell Mama."

"She'll say I was driven to it. She knows what a pest you

17

are. I'll tell her you were late for lunch and she'll give you such a wigging and I'll witness it." Orlando's contentment was disturbed by a distant rumbling. "Is that thunder? Should we change plans and get back to the hotel?"

"Hm? Sorry, I was miles away." Jonty's face suddenly paled. "Yes, it might be as well. Given the weather."

Thunderstorms. They still affected Jonty, always making him go "somewhere else"—a strange, lingering reaction to awful events in his formative years. At boarding school he'd been raped by two of the older boys, the first time being on a thundery night. Now that the guilty parties were all dead, Orlando had hoped his lover would be rid of the effect of storms, cured by his love, kindness and patience. But he wasn't, a fact that made Orlando feel even more of a failure.

He'd have given anything to be Jonty's Aesculapius rather than his Galatea.

Chapter Two

Tuesday evening after the rain had passed, the Bath Stone buildings shone like Welsh gold in the evening sun. Jonty and Orlando strolled languidly across Pulteney Bridge, sauntering past the Abbey and the Old Baths. When Jonty pointed out some of the wonderful places he'd found over the last few days, Orlando was genuinely amazed at the amount of local knowledge "Bard-pants" had acquired, although he suspected a lot of it had been cribbed from the Red Guide.

One place the Red Guide didn't mention Jonty had found all by himself. An unpromising-looking building hidden away behind the more glamorous establishments, it bore an ugly, unmarked door. Once opened, this led into a splendid marble atrium which formed the heart of Dr. Buckner's House of Sulis. Here was a place a chap could benefit from the therapeutic qualities of the natural hot springs without being annoyed by the female of the species. Strictly a "gentlemen only" institution, both in terms of gender and social standing, the baths had a reputation among the "quality", almost as select an institution as the Savile Row tailor's which had created Orlando's suit.

The House of Sulis was still open, even at this comparatively late hour, catering as it did for men of business as well as those of leisure. The two visitors accordingly poked their noses around the door to be greeted by a discreet yet welcoming chap with immaculate manners, who gave the impression of being a former batman or gentleman's gentleman.

"Dr. Stewart," the man said, bowing slightly. "I'm afraid that it's a little late to be starting a bathing session..."

"Ah, Millar. I only intended to show my colleague Dr. Coppersmith what a wonderful place this is."

"Oh, I'm sorry, sir. Please come in and make yourselves at home." Millar made a welcoming gesture. "Do you wish me to show you where all the facilities are?"

"No, I think I can remember them all from my previous visits. But if we need help, perhaps we could prevail upon you...?"

"My pleasure, sir."

The concierge discreetly withdrew, leaving Jonty to point out the marvels of the statuary and lead Orlando to the rooms where they could take the waters, either by drinking or immersion.

"Just how did you get yourself recognized here? You're a marvel. We've been in Bath five minutes and already you're a well-known figure." Orlando shook his head at his lover's temerity.

"Nothing to my especial credit this time. My father knows this place. *His* father used to come here for his rheumatism and brought Papa from a boy. I came very occasionally in my youth, so it seemed natural to see if it was still here." Jonty opened a door to reveal a strikingly designed room in the classical style but without pretensions to being really Roman. Its centrepiece was a steaming bath, from which slightly pungent odours arose—there was one occupant, an elderly fellow who nodded to them amiably and continued his soak. "One can bathe here or in the frigidarium, which really is freezing cold, so avoid it at all costs. You can sit in the steam room, Grandfather used to like that, or even drink the water, although it tastes like the contents of St. Thomas's fountain."

"You have experience of that ghastly sewer too, I presume." Orlando grinned. "And where does one change?"

"Along here." Jonty pointed to a door along the side wall of the room. "It can be accessed through there, or from the atrium. The changing room links everything, really, although this place can resemble a bit of a labyrinth unless you're sure of where you are."

"I'd like to take the opportunity of bathing at some point."

"We'll do so tomorrow morning if you wish—before breakfast, if that fits your plans."

"Will it be open then?"

"Of course. That's often a busy time, people starting the day with an invigorating sweat. Might interfere with getting breakfast though." Jonty looked rueful. Orlando was well aware he needed to start the day getting outside of a huge cup of tea, and something else to bank up the inner fires, in order to face the rigours ahead.

"Excuse me sir," Millar interposed in a diplomatic voice, "but we could provide you with some tea and a rack of toast."

"We don't want to put you to any trouble." Orlando was rather disappointed at the choice of drink on offer and would rather not indulge if Earl Grey was the only beverage available. He regarded it as a drink fit only for the epicene or invalid.

"Oh, it would be no trouble at all—it's a service we often provide for our gentlemen who have a tight schedule. I could produce a pot of coffee if that would be more to your taste."

Orlando's view softened. It had to be coffee in the morning, hot and strong. While he anticipated that the temperature and strength would probably be acceptable, he had no great hopes

21

for the quality, although this couldn't overcome the appeal of the hot bath. He nodded agreement. "Coffee would be excellent, thank you."

"I suppose that some nice bramble jelly wouldn't be in the offing to smear on that toast?" Jonty was hopeful although not confident. Orlando could live on bread and butter but *he* needed something to set him up for the day, if he couldn't get bacon.

"No bramble jelly, sir. However, there's a very nice pot or two of greengage conserve and some of this year's strawberry. It's not as good as the 1906 vintage, but not bad."

"Greengage it is. We'll see you in the morning, Mr. Millar."

The walk back to the Grand was so brisk a nightcap in a corner of the lounge bar felt the right end to a pleasant evening. The visit to the baths had made Jonty nostalgic—all the way home he'd been regaling his friend with tales of his paternal grandfather and maternal great uncles, who had been firm friends when they were younger. They'd been the originators of many a high-spirited lark, the direct cause of Richard Stewart and Helena Forster meeting, and consequently the source of Jonty's existence. The conversation had naturally turned to his grandmother, who was the indirect cause of Orlando's change in financial fortunes.

"Did your grandmother wear these?" Orlando fingered his little sapphire cufflinks, the only part of the old countess's jewellery which hadn't been sold and one that now was in a very different form from its original earring incarnation.

"She did. Every Christmas, as I remember." Jonty smiled happily—those gems evinced such fond memories.

"What was she like?"

"Mama without the right hook. She was lovely, such a grand and dignified lady and a great beauty in her youth, I'm told. Every eligible male made a beeline for Antonia Dewberry."

"That's where you get it from." Orlando was pleased to see his lover blush, even after all this time. And equally pleased they'd found a very quiet nook where such indiscretions could be uttered.

"Muffin. Anyway, for all that she hobnobbed with the great and good she still had time for her favourite little Jontykins. She would sit me next to her on the chesterfield and we'd play cards or word games, then she'd feed me Dundee cake and sips of eggnog when Papa wasn't looking."

"I wish I'd met her." It wasn't just a pleasantry. Orlando adored all the Stewarts to some extent or other and he'd have loved to have met Helena's mother. If only to compare the two formidable matrons.

"She'd have eaten you with a spoon. You'd have been given whole glasses of eggnog and asked things about differential equations and made to feel like the most important person in the world."

"You loved her very much, didn't you?" The lump which had suddenly appeared in Orlando's throat made it hard to force out his words.

"I did." Jonty discreetly undid a shirt button then reached beneath the material to find his crucifix. "She died within months of giving me this. I still miss the old girl."

Orlando wished he could reach over and finger the little gold trinket. "That necklace brings back such memories."

Jonty closed his fingers around it, smiling as he too, no doubt, recalled happy times sprawled before the log fires of St. Bride's. "How about Grandmamma Coppersmith down at Margate? What was she like?"

"Not as grand or glamorous as your grandmother, but at seven I thought the world of her. She was rather stern and

23

fierce to her servants and she always carried that great black bag I told you about, yet she was surprisingly kind to me. Much more so than my parents were."

Jonty lightly touched his lover's arm. "She used to take you paddling?"

"Indeed. She'd hold my hand as we walked down the beach and then if I'd been very good she would let me dabble my feet." He smiled in fond remembrance. "And she used to buy me sweeties. That's where I got my penchant for bullseyes, I suspect."

"Did she really? I never would have guessed."

"She was really very nice to me, much to father's annoyance." The familiar cloud associated with his parents crossed Orlando's mind. "He always said that it was unfair— he'd never been bought sweets."

"They often say that people can be more indulgent as grandparents than as parents. Perhaps there's not the pressure there is to be perfect in front of your offspring. And you can give the little tykes back to their rightful owners when you're tired of them." Jonty smiled, a sight which always consoled his friend.

"Your Mama and Papa seem kind enough."

"Oh they are. They're the exception that proves, by which I mean tests, the rule. But I do still wish that I could be Jontykins to Grandma again. Just for one more glass of eggnog."

📖

Wednesday began well, a mist in the air looking as if it would soon burn off and allow another glorious day to break through. Jonty and Orlando shivered slightly as they made their way to the baths but once through the door, the warmth—

both from the waters and from the fires which kept the changing rooms temperate in the early morning—cheered them.

"What are these?" Orlando held up what looked like rugby shorts, but made from finest silk.

"They're drawers *provided by the management for the wearing of in the pool,* as our old nanny used to say." Jonty deftly slipped into his pair.

"Might I ask why?"

"Because her father had been in the army and *he* always spoke like that."

"No, not that, idiot. Why the drawers? We're all gentlemen here, surely we can bathe as nature intended?"

"Dr. Coppersmith! Mama would make you wash your mouth out." Jonty grinned then sat down to watch the show. Orlando getting dressed or undressed was always amusing, if stimulating. "Old Dr. Buckner insisted his clientele dress in what he felt was an appropriate manner and when his son took over the establishment he's carried on the tradition. You can lounge in no more than a towel in the steam room, but the baths and frigidarium require sensible clothing, so none of your going *au naturel.*" He stopped, drumming his fingers on the bench in thought. "There was a scandal about it, I'm sure."

"About me not wanting to wear drawers?" Orlando, stripped down to his underwear, waved the garments in question like a flag.

"No, back in the 1880s when old Buckner was away undertaking research at Baden Baden or some other place with a silly name. In his absence the acting manager, who had modern ideas, allowed nude bathing. The House of Sulis acquired an unenviable reputation, with the temporary loss of some distinguished clientele."

"The Stewarts took up their drawers and walked, did they?"

25

Orlando slipped out of his own underwear and into the silk bathers with hardly an inch of inappropriate flesh exposed.

"You'll find yourself solving your own murder if you're not careful. You can imagine the furore—it took a lot of effort and diplomacy to regain the trust of the better quality of customers. Luckily there were miraculous cures effected by the waters on some members of the royal family and this place got re-established as *the* place to take the waters if you were a male of breeding and pedigree." Jonty pointed to himself to indicate he fell into this category. "And their guests of course. Ow."

"You deserved a whack for that. Now come on, I want to get into the water."

They languished in the baths, letting the heat and steam relax every muscle, breathing in the strange but therapeutic fumes. Fifteen minutes of wallowing made them feel like new men. The coffee and toast effected an even more potent change, the former being a far superior brew to anything they had found in Bath so far.

"This is almost as good as Mrs. Ward's." Orlando sipped his coffee appreciatively.

"That's a compliment to be savoured. You should tell Millar." It was a compliment without precedent, Orlando having always sworn that no one in the world could make coffee that came anywhere near the brew the housekeeper to Forsythia Cottage, their house back in Cambridge, could produce.

"We should come here as often as we can." Orlando finished his last sip of coffee, looking hopefully into the cup in case he'd missed a drop or two.

"I'm happy to do that." Jonty pushed away his plate. "Righty ho, pleasure has to give way to work. I need to hunt out some Tudor literature which I'm told is to be found in an obscure bookshop, if I can achieve what I've failed at the last few days and actually find the place."

"We'll meet for lunch?"

"Yes, as long as you'll let yourself be taken up to Ralph Allen's castle afterwards, to look at the preparations for the play. The manager of the company's going to be there—I need to meet him and confirm my involvement with the production."

"He's probably heard of you and will refuse to let you anywhere near it." Orlando cuffed Jonty's shoulder in parting. "Maybe he'd find me more useful."

"You can always suggest what type of tree I wear for Birnham Wood. Just your sort of thing."

📖

"Stewart? Jonty Stewart?"

An attractive American brogue split the air, making the men spin around. They'd been standing admiring Ralph Allen's folly and watching the activity surrounding it. The rudiments of a stage was going up, business being worked out at the same time, groups of people rehearsing scenes or looking at properties. It had made an amusing scene and they weren't prepared for interruption.

"Harding! What the deuce are you doing here?"

"Putting on a play, of course."

"You're producing the Shakespeare here? The Scottish play?"

"Say it—say *Macbeth*. Surely you don't believe in that old chestnut about it being unlucky?" The newcomer smiled, an expression which was immediately mirrored by Jonty.

"*Macbeth* it is, then."

"Good. Don't you dare say it around the rest of the

27

company, though. They're all infected with the usual superstitions. I have to refer to 'himself' as the Thane or some other euphemism—I need someone I can talk to without the nonsense or I'll go mad." He grinned again.

"You're not going to play Macbeth yourself, surely?" Jonty, almost dancing with delight, waved eagerly at the stage.

"No, I'll be Banquo. And I'm producing, of course." The actor swept his hand around, encompassing all the properties and players.

Orlando could stay silent no longer. "Am I to be introduced?"

"I'm so sorry." Jonty touched his arm, lightly. "Dr. Coppersmith, this is Mr. Harding. Jimmy, this is Orlando."

Orlando felt bad enough that he'd been ignored, left out of this obviously happy meeting, but for Jonty to break one of their cardinal rules was scandalous. He'd used Christian names in public and they weren't on holiday, or hadn't declared themselves as being so yet. He could feel the hackles rising, a knot of anger moving up his spine. "Pleased to meet you, Dr. Harding."

"*Mr.* Harding."

"My apologies, *Mister* Harding." If Orlando had openly said *I don't like you or your smarmy face, go away and leave us alone,* his feelings couldn't have been plainer.

"We were at University College together." Jonty had picked up the ice in his lover's tone and sought to smooth the situation with pleasantries. "Jimmy studied English literature at home, in America, then came over to improve his already considerable knowledge of the Bard. Now he runs his own productions on both sides of the Atlantic." He looked uneasily from one man to the other, knowing he'd committed a terrible social *faux pas* in not introducing them straightaway. In the sheer delight of

28

seeing his old friend all decorum had fled from his brain.

"They told me there was some guy from Cambridge who'd been lurking about and offering his services..."

Orlando bridled at the unflattering description of what Jonty had been doing. Only *he* was allowed to make fun of or criticise the man.

"I'd have never in a million years guessed it was you." Harding smiled, the genuine pleasure he felt at seeing his old acquaintance again shining through.

"You don't mind the prospect of me hanging around getting under everyone's feet?"

"Not at all. I'm sure you'll put me right on all my mistakes of interpretation. You were always pretty hot about the nitty-gritty of production. And we'll have to find you a part to play." A huge grin crossed the American's face. "Lady Macbeth will need a handmaiden or two. Fancy being a traditional player?"

Luckily, Orlando didn't catch this remark, his mind being full of visions involving his fist and Harding's face.

"Not my cup of tea, I'm afraid." Jonty laughed but couldn't shake off his discomfort. "I'll be the porter if you need one, or else just a part of Birnham Wood."

"I'll see what I can work out. Will you join me for dinner? Both of you?" Harding added as an afterthought.

"Not tonight, I'm afraid. Tomorrow perhaps?"

"It's a deal then. Come and watch us practise tomorrow, though. I'd like your input on the *Out damned spot* bit."

Jonty nodded. "Tomorrow then."

Harding smiled and held out his hand to Jonty to be shaken. "Excellent." He offered Orlando his hand as well. The man grasped it grudgingly.

Jonty strode down the hill. He could sense Orlando's unease—anyone not completely oblivious would have—and felt the need to be away from the makeshift theatre, getting a chance to clear his mind. Jimmy Harding had been a pleasant enough young man back in the London days, but somehow in the intervening three years he'd matured, like a wine or cheese which gradually reaches the peak of its perfection. He *had* been agreeable, now he was gorgeous. Heart-stoppingly gorgeous.

Realising this simple fact caused a curious and unsettling sensation in Jonty's brain. The last two years he'd had eyes for Orlando alone and now he'd been "brought up with a round turn", as his papa might term it when at his most extravagantly eloquent. The sheer charisma of Harding had knocked all the social proprieties out of Jonty's noddle, threatening to reduce him to a gibbering wreck if he didn't take a close rein on himself.

The horse-drawn two-seater cab that had brought them up the hill was waiting for them, Jonty having insisted they retain it. Orlando wasn't as talkative for the journey back down to the Grand as he'd been coming up.

"What is eating you, Orlando?" Jonty could have answered the question easily enough, but he wanted the air cleared.

"How well did you know him in London?" The inquisition started.

"Jimmy? We knew each other for a couple of years at University College." Jonty looked out the window, at the floor, avoided Orlando's gaze. "Met at lectures, naturally, and then we discovered we were members of the same club. His father had arranged his membership, so he'd have an easier time of it when he first came over. Not that Jimmy finds it hard to make friends."

"I can see that. Very easy going. Have you kept in touch?"

"Just cards at Christmas, with a few words of news. Thought you'd have spotted them on the old mantelpiece in my set of rooms at St. Bride's." Jonty kept his tone light and easy, yet inside the prickles of tetchiness were breaking out.

"I don't go through your post, sir."

"Orlando, whatever is the matter?" Jonty grabbed his lover's hand, turning to face him for the first time in the journey.

"Isn't it supposed to be *Dr. Coppersmith* in public? We aren't on holiday."

Jonty could feel his blood starting to boil—this was all getting so bloody silly. "I've declared it holiday time, *Orlando*. Now would you be so kind as to tell me what's bothering you? You've been like a bear with a migraine ever since Harding hove into view."

"I don't like him."

"Oh, is it Mr. Ainslie all over again? Afraid he's going to take you off behind the castle and ravish you?"

Orlando didn't reply. Clenched hands and muttered, indistinct words made any reply unnecessary.

"Well, is it?" The truth suddenly dawned. "Or do you think he's going to take *me* off and ravish me?" Jonty didn't need to wait for an answer. The pathetic look of feigned innocence on Orlando's face was enough to tell him all he needed to know. "Maybe you think he's already done that, back in London and that I somehow neglected to tell you? Oh sorry, Orlando, it wasn't just you and Richard Marsters I've been to bed with, I had Jimmy as well. And Clive and Gerald and Francis and the entire second fifteen. What sort of man do you think I am?"

He tapped on the roof to get the cab to stop, then stepped out, ignoring Orlando's sudden shocked protest—not a voiced one but a hand firmly grabbing his arm.

"I may see you later, Dr. Coppersmith. Or maybe not." Jonty slammed the door shut and made his way off into the crowd.

Chapter Three

Orlando sat in the hotel room quietly cursing himself—the last hour had been a catalogue of errors and all of them his fault. Why on earth had he accused his lover, or to all intents and purposes accused him, of being unfaithful with Harding? Jonty hadn't even known Orlando at the time he'd last seen the man in question, so technically he couldn't be guilty of adulterous behaviour even if a liaison *had* occurred. And what evidence had he based these accusations on? The horribly condemning facts that Jonty had been a bit free and easy with their Christian names and had, for once, not quite observed the proprieties of social etiquette.

Orlando put his head in his hands, moaning theatrically even though no one was there to hear him. It all seemed so stupid now, as he recalled all they'd said, then analysed every word for its meaning. Jonty had just been displaying his usual friendly character, genuinely pleased to be meeting an old friend, and he'd acted like a big soppy schoolgirl, all pouting jealousy. One who needed a slapping.

Then to have crowned all the idiocy by going and misplacing Jonty in the crowd. He'd been a fraction too slow in getting out of the coach, half his mind on throwing some money at the cabman, only to find he'd lost sight of that golden head in the throng. Jonty had never gone off before. And the only time he'd threatened it—after an argument over some shrubs, for heaven's sake—Orlando had reminded him that Mrs. Stewart would give him a piece of her mind should he turn up on her doorstep. Then she'd tie the little beast up until he came to claim him.

Wandering the streets, hoping to catch a glimpse of his lover, his anger had soon dissipated to be replaced by panic. What if Jonty just took off somewhere? The thought that he might take himself straight off to Harding flitted through Orlando's brain but was soon dispatched as being too uncomfortable for consideration.

Logic eventually reasserted itself, as Orlando quartered the area around the Abbey. Jonty would have to return to the hotel for all his things, so that was where he had to go and station himself. When the shocking thought occurred to him *en route* that his friend might just decide to leave all his things behind, along with his discarded lover, Orlando ignored that, too.

But Jonty was not, and had not been, back at the Grand. Now Orlando was beginning to despair of him ever appearing; if there'd been sackcloth and ashes to hand, then he would have indulged in them. No one wanted him to do detecting, he couldn't cure Jonty, and now he'd even failed at keeping a hold on his lover.

He was beating himself about the proverbial head, if not the literal one, when the door creaked slightly and a familiar tread came over the threshold. Orlando swung around, leapt up, then bounded over to his lover. "Jonty, please forgive me. I was stupid and I won't blame you if you decide to shout or punch me. But I beg you not to leave me."

Jonty shook his head. "I was never going to leave you, I just needed some time to calm down, you should know me by now."

"I bet you're fuming with me. I was completely wrong saying

those things, I never meant to be so hard. This stupid disagreement is all my fault, I'm sorry." The words tumbled out randomly, pouring all Orlando's emotions with them.

"If there's any more of this I'll start calling you Dr. Hairshirt. In the Senior Common Room if need be." Jonty grinned.

"Don't joke, it isn't funny. I was worried sick."

"I'm a grown man, Orlando. I wasn't going to come to any harm walking the streets for an hour." The grin turned itself off.

"You might have if you'd gone back to the folly."

"And what precisely do you mean by that?" The grin had become an icy, thin-lipped glare.

Orlando didn't dare answer. If he'd got it all wrong, Jonty really would kill him and if he'd got it right, Jonty would be off again like a shot.

"I'm waiting."

"I think I misunderstood what was going on up there, when we talked to Harding. I made some rash assumptions." Orlando studied his shoes, but they didn't reassure him.

"You certainly did." The icy edge in Jonty's voice eased into weariness. "Look here, Jimmy was only ever a friend, I promise you. He meant nothing more to me than Lavinia's Ralph does." Jonty leaned up to kiss his lover's brow. "Now shut up about it. We need to get changed for dinner or else there'll be nothing left except stale bread and rancid butter."

They might now be lacking a turn of pace on the rugby pitch, but getting into dinner jackets Orlando and Jonty could tackle like sprinters. They did justice to the rack of lamb, although conversation over dinner was a bit stilted, but the port over coffee, taken sitting in the lounge, loosened their tongues. It seemed, for the moment, as if the whole incident regarding

Harding had never happened. Or maybe it was just too painful to refer to at present.

A muffled wailing coming from the street outside drew them to look out of the window. A small, obviously spoiled boy was leading his keeper a merry dance. Orlando wasn't impressed. His experience of children was admittedly limited to the smaller Stewarts, all of whom had beautiful manners even if they were high spirited, and all of whom were given appropriate discipline when the situation demanded.

"That child should be given as good a spanking as Mama gave you." For the first time since lunch, Jonty's voice has its old spark of mischief.

Orlando grimaced. When they'd broken their journey at the Stewarts' home, Jonty's mother had walloped his backside for nothing worse than dosing her husband with an experimental analgesic powder. All purely in the interests of science and not appreciated by his hostess. "I suspect I still bear the mark. I can certainly feel the imprint of her hand even now, if I lie awkwardly."

"That has to be the most blatant lie. It was days ago." Jonty signalled for the waiter to refill their glasses. The memory alone deserved two ports.

"It may well have been days, but I swear that I'll carry the scars, emotional and physical, to my dying day."

"You are wonderfully dramatic. Have you considered offering to play Lady Macbeth?"

Why on earth did Jonty have to mention that wretched play again? Just when Orlando had got his thoughts away from handsome, smarmy Americans and onto happier times. "The less said about that hussy, the better." He yawned, equally theatrically. "I need my bed."

"So do I. I could sleep for a week."

The fact that Jonty obviously meant the sentiment, that he wasn't acting a part in public, left Orlando both disappointed and unnerved.

📖

Despite what he'd said, Jonty couldn't sleep. Normally his head would hit the pillow and he'd be oblivious until dawn, yet tonight he couldn't locate the magic switch to turn off consciousness. In truth he was feeling rather uncomfortable, not at his display of petulance on the way home from the folly— something he felt was justified in the face of an accusation of disloyalty—but at some of the thoughts which had been flitting through his own brain this last hour.

Jimmy Harding had attracted him enormously. That simple fact had been a great shock. There was a whole raft of guilt loading him down concerning this man's animal magnetism, or whatever it was. Jonty had never looked at any other man since he'd met Orlando, had never wanted to, yet he'd have been happy to look at Harding all afternoon. It was wrong, Jonty knew it was, and earlier he'd wrestled with a tangle of emotions as he'd wandered around the city or sat in the gardens deep in thought. How could he in all honesty be cross at Orlando when he'd hit so near to the truth of things?

He watched the dawn gradually infiltrate Thursday morning's sky, trying to focus on the delights of the day ahead rather than a pair of inviting blue eyes. The weather promised to be overcast and dreary, although there was bathing to look forward to. They'd made the decision to take the waters at the House of Sulis every day they could and, the coffee having proved so superior, they chose to breakfast there again this morning. *It'll be for the best, as long as I don't end up falling asleep in the water.*

"Dr. Stewart. How is your father?" Dr. Buckner the younger came forward as the men entered the hallway of the baths, holding out his hand for Jonty to shake it. He'd been delighted to hear about the man's visit, and was eager to renew acquaintance with a member of one of his establishment's oldest families.

"Dr. Buckner, how marvellous to see you again. I think I was hardly out of my teens when we last met." Jonty wouldn't have recognised the man, he looked so careworn.

"That would be right, sir. It's been far too long." Buckner turned his attention to Orlando. "Would it be presumptuous to ask if this is Dr. Coppersmith?"

"It would not, indeed." Jonty grinned at the discomfort this innocent remark produced in his lover.

Orlando bridled. "And would it be presumptuous of me to ask how you guessed my name?"

"I read the article Mr. Stewart wrote in *The Times*, about the Woodville Ward case. I'm afraid that your reputations preceded you." Buckner suddenly stopped, looked intently at Orlando. "Are you in Bath on university business? Or is it more a matter of, shall we say, *constabulary duty*?"

"Mainly the former. Dr. Coppersmith has some books and documents to inspect. I'm here for a working holiday, wrestling with an unruly manuscript, although I'm afraid I've found something else to keep me out of mischief, poking my nose in with the theatre company up at the folly." Jonty spoke the last bit quickly, still feeling his way about the subject of Harding, who, he remembered with trepidation, would be meeting them for a meal later.

"So would you be at all interested in—" Buckner lowered his voice, quite needlessly as they were the only people present in the hallway, "—a little case of unsolved murder?"

Jonty was very fond of *Henry V* and particularly liked the line about greyhounds in the slips—it could have been applied to Orlando right at that moment. It seemed as though his ears had pricked up and his nostrils were aquiver.

"Shouldn't the police be involved?" Orlando was clearly fighting the temptation to say "show us the body now, we're your men"

"They were and they showed no real interest in getting to the bottom of things. It happened a while ago now, back when my father was abroad. Not a happy time for the House of Sulis."

"I remember the stories. Father told me of the days when this place had acquired *a reputation*."

Buckner shuddered at the thought. "Twenty-five years ago, it must be—1882—yet for many of us it seems like only yesterday." He passed a hand over his brow. "Take the waters, gentlemen, please, then consider whether you have the time or inclination to listen to a very sad and mysterious story."

Jonty smiled at the melodramatic tone. "We will. Shall we meet you over coffee and tell you our decision?" Buckner nodded, leaving the fellows of Bride's to make their way to the changing rooms, Jonty rightfully confident that he knew what his friend's answer would be.

"We have time to take it on, Jonty. I only work for half the day, really, and I bet I could concertina that if I tried. You're not doing anything much."

"Hold on. I know I can finish the book soon enough, once I get the last bit clear in my mind, but I promised to help with that play. Might even get a little part in it." Jonty really did want to be one of the trees in Birnham Wood.

"Even that won't take you all your time. And this might be far more important, anyway, than *Macbeth*. We can work out some logistics…"

Jonty felt guilty enough over the Harding incident to agree without further argument. Maybe he could get wrapped up enough in this case to forget the man up at the folly.

📖

Buckner had coffee, tea and a selection of preserves to spread on their toast ready and waiting. Once the inner men were being filled he started to lay out the skeleton of the sad tale. In the time when his father had been away in Europe, the man who'd been in charge of the bathhouse had soon let things go astray, to the extent of encouraging nude bathing, which he felt was natural and healthy. Inevitably advantage had been taken of this, and private bookings made where outrageous parties occurred at the pool.

"It caused such a scandal." Buckner shook his head. "I can remember to this day my father's ire at returning to find his temple of health had been made into a whoremonger's den."

"I suggest that Dr. Coppersmith might like to cover his ears at this point." Jonty grinned at his friend. "We may be discussing matters of which he is in ignorance."

"You will excuse Dr. Stewart, sir. I believe his mother dropped him on his head when he was a child and he's never fully recovered his faculties."

Buckner smiled, a look of amusement crossing his face for the first time. "Ah, you take me back. The Forster brothers enjoyed bantering with each other when they were young men. Your father too, Dr. Stewart. That was after…" The smile disappeared. "At the time of these parties I referred to there was great scandal—nude bathing with both sexes freely mixing, then all sorts of things going on in the other rooms. How it was ever allowed, I don't know, but I dare say that if you grease enough palms then anything can be sanctioned. Things came to a head when my father returned unexpectedly right at the end of one of these—" he lowered his voice, "—orgies. He quickly cleared the place out, or so he thought, then took to task the man who had let the place go to wrack and ruin. I suspect he may have horsewhipped him although I've never verified the fact. He soon re-established his own rule and regulations. The next morning he organised a squadron of cleaners to scrub the entire place clean of any trace of the previous clientele. One of the women involved found a body."

Orlando, who'd been slowly assimilating the information and compartmentalising it in his head for future reference, looked up abruptly from his toast buttering as Buckner stopped in full flow. "A body? Where?"

"In the little side room off the frigidarium, where we kept towels and the like. No one had thought to check there when all the rats had been swept out the previous night. They found a young woman dressed only in her underclothing and looking as if she'd been dead some hours."

"Did the police find out who she was?"

"Yes—a lady of the night, not to put too fine a point on it. There had been several of them present at the party the night before and word soon got around. Her name was quickly established as Sarah Carter."

"Was no one brought to book for the crime?" Jonty looked up from his fourth slice of toast.

"There was no investigation. They declared that she died of natural causes, the effect of taking a very cold bath immediately after a hot one, and the case was closed."

"But you did specify earlier on that this was an unsolved murder." Jonty frowned, the corner of his tongue slipping out of his mouth as he concentrated on the information being given to him.

"It is, or so my father believed. He'd seen the body, had made an initial examination and was certain she had bruising to her neck, enough to suggest strangulation."

"Then why was the cause of death given as accidental?" Orlando felt everything seemed off track here. There was no logic to the suppression of facts.

Buckner took a long draught of coffee, then shrugged. "The usual story. The girl had neither family nor particular friends willing to speak up for her, whereas those others who had been present at the—I cannot avoid the word—*debauchery* included men of influence and power. They didn't want their sordid adventures being made public and so they swept it all under the carpet."

"Didn't your father raise the hue and cry? He must have suspected from the start." Orlando waved his knife, as if he were a judge with his gavel, about to question an obstinate witness.

"He did, but he had the reestablishment of the good name of the baths to consider. Any hint of further scandal might have meant the end of all that he'd worked to build up. I can see the look of disapproval in your eye and I know that you'll think him exactly what he thought himself, a moral coward. Believe me, he couldn't have caused a fuss, he would have been ruined."

"So why raise the matter now? Twenty-five years isn't like four hundred—there will still be people alive who were there that night, I'm sure." Orlando laid down the knife, chastened.

"My father died only two years ago and his final days were racked with guilt that he hadn't acted to avenge the young girl.

He made me promise that if the opportunity presented itself I would take the step he'd failed to." Buckner looked at each man in turn, eyes imploring. "Will you take the commission?"

"Is there enough to work on, so many years later? Have we a hope of succeeding?" Orlando tried to temper his natural excitement with a pragmatic stance.

"I believe so. I'll share all that my father accumulated, including lists of names. I wouldn't have asked if I didn't have a degree of hope."

Orlando cast a discreet look at his lover. "Then we are your men." It was wonderful to be given a case again, to have someone believe he was worth consulting. And the thought that a nice murder investigation might keep Jonty away from Jimmy Harding was a positive bonus to the case.

Chapter Four

Jonty settled down in his suite with a jug of orange juice, a plate of biscuits and a sheaf of paper. He found distinct echoes of the Woodville Ward case here, although this time the documents weren't a ragged assortment of bits and pieces, some of which needed decoding. This was far more simple, the things they'd got to hand being all the work of one man and containing a lucid, logical explanation of the events at the House of Sulis.

The first part of the narrative featured a bold copperplate hand, a clear account written at the time of what had transpired the evening of Sarah Carter's death, and then another explanation concerning what the authorities had said happened. The two were not the same.

The second part was in a slightly less steady form of the same hand, but a similar lucidity applied to the story it told. Dr. Buckner had obviously never lost his faculties, although his tone had changed. This was a man who obviously felt great guilt that he hadn't pursued matters more vigorously at the time of what, he was certain, was a cold-blooded murder. He felt that he'd let the victim down, when he might have been the only person to be her champion and see justice done.

Jonty's process was simple—he skimmed through the papers, getting an overall picture before he read them again more carefully and made some notes. He smiled as he did so, reflecting how cross Orlando had been that he wasn't to get first access to these intriguing documents. He would be head down over his mathematical tomes, although Jonty would have bet a fiver that at least half the man's mind would be on what was contained in these documents. Well, Orlando would get his turn in the afternoon, when Jonty went to poke his nose in the vicinity of the Scottish play, but he'd have stolen the march on his lover.

Jonty's notes started with what little was known of the victim, knowledge which was patchy at best. Sarah, a lady of the night who worked on her own rather than in some establishment, was known to one or two other girls who'd been present at the baths that evening, although they weren't clear on her history. She'd appeared in Bath quite suddenly, she'd been popular with the more sophisticated gentlemen, she had nice manners and a pretty face, she appeared to have no family. And that was about it. One of her fellow prostitutes had identified her at what passed for an inquest and this woman had told Buckner what little else she knew.

The list of those who had allegedly been using the facilities at the House of Sulis on the night—all of whom were inclined to deny the fact at the time—made Jonty whistle. He wondered what his papa would make of it all; it would certainly add more fuel to his constant fire of battle against adulterers and whoremongers. The sight of one of his wife's ex-suitors on the list made a rise in Mr. Stewart's blood pressure even more likely.

Little sprang to the eye in terms of clues, though. According to Buckner, the girl had been throttled—according to the official view she had died of heart failure. The doctor said that a number of so-called gentlemen of various ages and standing had been present at the baths, along with a handful of ladies of loose morals. The police stated that only the prostitutes had been present, although they never bothered to explain why the girls should have been there on their own. The only thing upon which both accounts seemed to agree was where Sarah had been laid to rest, a little church to the east of the city where Buckner had arranged for her to have a decent Christian burial. Jonty put it on his list of places to visit.

In his notebook he made an inventory of things to do—visiting all who'd been named as present was the first—then decided he'd read enough and needed to see the grave *now*. His excuse was that he wanted fresh air, but in reality his mind felt befuddled by the bald information and lack of clues. He found a cab and set off for Bathampton.

He found the grave eventually, with the aid of Mr. White, the verger, who was lurking in the vicinity. The old man assured him they had many a visitor in July, especially when they celebrated their flower festival and the church was ablaze with floral arrangements. Jonty had dreaded this white-haired, toothless man nabbing him, yet he proved amusing, knowledgeable and, most importantly, he remembered Sarah Carter, or at least her funeral. Jonty explained who he was, also slipping in who his father and grandfathers were, emphasising the fact he'd been asked to look into what "people" believed was a mysterious death that hadn't been investigated in sufficient detail at the time. If he implied that those people were in fact his relatives, that elasticity with the truth was just part of his detecting job.

Mr. White took his guest into the vestry to show him both the register and a map of the graveyard which he'd prepared only the year before. Sarah's grave was tucked away in a corner, the least fashionable part of this particular God's little acre. As they studied the documents and admired the fine brasses in the church, the verger chattered away. "Only Dr.

Buckner and his son bothered to turn up at the graveside—they'd given the poor girl a proper send-off, not some pauper's burial. None of her friends came to pay their respects, although I expect the old rector would have seen them off if they'd dared show up, he not even approving of Mary Magdalene..."

They reached the graveside, where a simple stone showed only the girl's name and that already partly covered with moss and lichen. The sight of fresh flowers on the plot cut Mr. White's narration short.

"Now, Dr. Stewart, that's an odd thing. A couple of times a year we get flowers appearing here but none of us ever sees who leaves them. Often they're white lilies which I'm certain must come from a hothouse."

"How intriguing." Jonty stopped to touch the delicate petals of the roses which graced the earth.

"And sometimes it's these lovely things. Which brings me back to that lass's funeral. Somebody sent a lovely floral tribute, but it didn't come from the doctor, he'd brought his own with him. This one had been left at the gate of the church with a note that it was for her, although it gave no name, no clue at all to who might have put it there. The arrangement was far too grand to come from one of her friends, not unless the girl knew someone who had elevated herself in society, as these women sometimes do."

"So somebody remembers her?"

"They do. And they must still hold that remembrance very dear to still be going to all this trouble."

"What did the original note say?"

"Very simple it was, sir. Just *Goodbye, my dear.*" The verger stooped down again to pick up a single red rose, handing it to Jonty. "I suspect you've been sent to be her avenger or champion or something. God always sees to things in the end.

Those mills might grind slow but they grind exceeding small. Keep this as a token of her and find out what the truth is."

Jonty was stunned to find that Sarah Carter had such an unexpected supporter.

"Where did you get the flower?" Orlando had only just arrived at the public house where they'd decided to take a sandwich for lunch and was surprised to see his lover alighting from a cab with a rose in his hand. He hoped the name Jimmy Harding had nothing to do with it.

"From an aged admirer." Jonty launched into the story of the books, the church and the verger, skipping about in time and chronology as was his wont, which drove Orlando mad. What irked him particularly was the fact that his friend had, as usual, made an unexpected breakthrough, or what might potentially be one. At least they would now have a concrete question or two to put to the people they met regarding this case. Flowers might also mean a florist and Jonty could be kept out of a lot of mischief by being dispatched to investigate them.

"While you're off explaining the exact meaning of act thingummy, scene whatsit to the strolling players, I can see if I can make contact with some of those listed as being present on the night Sarah Carter died." Orlando held the rose up to the light, as if it held the clue to the whole mystery.

"Wouldn't you have more fun seeing if some of the ladies of loose morals are still in the vicinity?" Jonty reclaimed his flower and lodged it in his buttonhole. "Although I suppose that by now they'd be blousy matrons or starchy grandmothers who are attempting to forget their shady pasts."

Orlando pooh-poohed this on the entirely logical grounds

that the more recent entries by Buckner had given addresses for some of the men, most of whom still seemed to be alive and several of whom were still in the district. He didn't confess that he hoped the women would never have to be consulted. He grudgingly agreed that they would fulfil their promise to Harding and entertain him at the Grand for dinner at seven thirty, if Jonty would remind the man of the invitation.

As it turned out, Jonty couldn't do this in person because Harding wasn't up at Ralph Allen's Sham Castle. There was a buzz of rumour and once Jonty had cut through the wittering and the speculation, he managed to establish that Jimmy had been summoned to see the city authorities. They'd been alarmed to hear that the production might not be seemly and wanted a full explanation. He'd gone off, cap in hand and on his best behaviour, to charm the great and good into letting the company carry on with its planned interpretation of the great play. He was said to have a name or two to drop of people who had guaranteed to attend the first night, names of such earth-shattering grandeur that any council would be unlikely to gainsay their entertainment.

It wasn't expected that he'd return that day so the message was sent via a small, seemingly reliable lad. Jonty was roped in to help with blocking out and attempting to direct some of the lesser scenes, an exercise which delighted him, especially when it came to the business with the porter. He had some vague notes in Jimmy's sprawling hand to act as a guide so he just crossed his fingers and hoped he didn't make an utter mess of things. If he ended up ruining the entertainment for the minor royals, his father would spifflicate him.

📖

Orlando had little luck to begin with. He'd chosen to visit a Mr. Bredon, simply on the grounds that he lived in Great Pulteney Street, which was convenient. It turned out Mr. Bredon was away in Bristol and not likely to return until the weekend, so he assayed a visit to the old Goats and Compasses public house, where Sarah Carter was said to have taken occasional lodgings, but that turned out to be a respectable pair of villas, the original building having burned down these fifteen years past.

Third time lucky proved a true saying for once. One of the names on the list of men who'd been seen at the House of Sulis rang a bell with Orlando, although he hadn't confessed the fact to Jonty—this visit was something he wanted to do on his own and then boast about afterwards. A small chill ran down his spine at the thought of a piece of detecting he'd done alone in their last case, but he ignored it.

He found the house in question easily, the address being listed in the more recent documents and at risk of only being a few years out of date. Buckner had obviously kept an eye, as much as he could, on the whereabouts of those involved in the unpleasantness at the House of Sulis and had made sure whoever was to take on this case had as much information as he could provide.

A pleasant-looking housekeeper answered the door, a woman obviously out of the same mould as the blessed Mrs. Ward. Orlando gave his name, asked for Dr. Keane, then was ushered into the hall to wait.

Dr Keane. The man had left Gabriel College, Oxford, in disgrace when the authorities found he'd been to London on occasions to frequent a house of ill repute. Orlando's old college had been a place of great moral rectitude (and quite possibly rampant hypocrisy) so the Dean had insisted on sending the man packing.

It would have surprised Jonty to know that Orlando hadn't been among those who'd been judgemental of the disgraced fellow. Keane had been his first tutor, teaching him elements of physics which had opened up new vistas in terms of applied mathematics. He'd been kind to a boy who felt very lost in Oxford and when he'd been sent off in ignominy Orlando had even uncharacteristically written him a letter, thanking Keane for his thoughtfulness. The reply had been equally gracious, greatly touching the shy, young undergraduate.

"Coppersmith! I should say Dr. Coppersmith, I'm sorry." Keane seemed to remember his old student with real affection, if his face was anything to go by. He plied Orlando with tea and scones, asked about his detecting (he too had seen the article in the *Times* which had given the two fellows of Bride's such notoriety) and only then enquired why he was paying a call.

The Orlando of his first investigation, nearly two years previously, would have become almost incoherent at this point, tripping over his tongue in an effort to find the right words. Now he not only had understanding and maturity under his belt but the experience of being with Jonty Stewart for the last two years. No one could be in the vicinity of that imp of fame and not be affected.

"Dr. Keane, I won't mince words. I respect you enormously and wish to be entirely candid. Dr. Stewart and I have been asked to investigate a death which took place twenty-five years ago, and we have good reason to believe that you might be able to help us."

"I will try my best, although twenty-five years is a long time and my memory isn't what it was." Keane grinned, although he hadn't shown any evidence of a falling-off of his faculties. He was in his early forties, Orlando guessed, yet seemed older, as if he'd become shrunken into his chair and rather prematurely wizened. He was handsome enough, even though his hair had thinned and the lines on his face were noticeable.

The shuddering realisation that this is how *he* might have turned out if Jonty hadn't come to steal his chair turned Orlando's stomach. He returned, disconcerted, to his notes. "It happened at the House of Sulis, the night the late Dr. Buckner returned and cleansed his temple."

Keane nodded. "I was there, I shan't deny it now, though I may have done at the time." His eyes lost focus, as if he were looking not at Orlando but back into the distant past. "They found a girl there, dead, the next day."

"Sarah Carter, yes."

"I had forgotten her name. But I never really knew her, even then. I would have been eighteen and about to head up to Oxford myself. I was taken along by a set of friends, several of whom were much older than me, to be given a sort of send-off. 'Condemned man eating a hearty meal,' they called it. I am not proud of what we did then—we were young, full of needs and lacking the willpower to simply ignore them. We thought we were so daring and so clever." Keane shook his head. "With the benefit of hindsight, I know we were merely idiots, as I was again at Cranmer." He cast a glance around the room. "I have a happy enough life here, I have independent means. I lack, however, the opportunity to talk to those of an equal academic rigour. I miss them, Dr. Coppersmith, the discussions in the Common Room, the debate with my fellow mathematicians."

"Did you never try to find another post?"

"I never wanted to be anywhere except Oxford. I made a mistake and paid for it heavily, sir. Please take my advice and never do the same." Keane sighed, his ashen face appearing ten years older.

"I promise you that I shall not." Orlando made a valid pledge—he would never be inclined to visit a doxy, male or female. Although he knew well enough that if anyone found out the truth about him and Jonty, they could easily use that knowledge to get the pair of them kicked out of St. Bride's. And straight into jail. "In return, will you promise to tell me all you know?"

"I shall. I can verify that the girl was present, indeed several women of her profession were there. She didn't associate with my crowd—she and a couple of friends were exclusively with another party who were also using the facilities, if you take my meaning."

"And did you have any idea who this other party were?" Despite the fact that Orlando had names, he wished to have an eyewitness answer the question. The relationships between all those present that night might prove crucial.

"No, I'm sorry. I can verify the addresses you have for my friends, those with whom I am still in contact, which might allow you to interview and eliminate them from your enquiries. The other men, however..." Keane shrugged.

"I know that none of your friends attended the girl's funeral, but do you know if any of them sent flowers? Or still do?"

Dr. Keane thought long, as if he were systematically going through all of his acquaintances to search for evidence. As Orlando might well have done in the same situation. "I wasn't aware that any of my party knew the girl, although that is not to say that they didn't. I remember the two women who entertained us—one of them I'm still on nodding terms with. If you needed to know where to find her, I could help."

"Thank you. If you could add that to my list of names I would be obliged. We are staying at the Grand if you think of anything else and wish to contact us. I'm afraid we haven't much time to make progress in this case and I'd be grateful for any assistance you could give."

📖

Jonty and Orlando were taking a small pre-prandial sherry in the bar when Jimmy Harding appeared, looking rather flushed.

"Gentlemen, I hope you will pardon me. I've had to run these last ten minutes so as not to be late." Jimmy beamed, looking from man to man as if expecting an immediate flurry of forgiveness.

"Did your meeting with the council go on so long?" Orlando's tone was as stony as his face.

Jimmy shook his head and grimaced. "No, not at all. Although it took a while for them all to turn up and then discuss for half an hour or so exactly *why* they were meeting."

"Sounds like a typical council. It can be like that at Bride's." Jonty sought to provide some warmth of welcome amid the glacial chill his lover emanated.

"It's like that anytime people meet with bees in their several bonnets. Once things got under way I persuaded them fairly quickly that we weren't about to engage in some lascivious production which would sully the morals of the good folk of Bath. And the fact that the Duke of Connaught is coming down to see our first night sort of tipped the balance." He signalled for the waiter, then ordered a glass of beer. "It was afterwards the trouble started. I got accosted, Jonty. Barely escaped alive."

Orlando started, horrified. "A physical assault, in broad daylight?"

Jimmy laughed. "No, that would have been a simple matter

of fisticuffs from which I could have made my escape merely bruised and battered. I was accosted by a woman."

"Some people would envy you that." Jonty smiled. He vaguely remembered a string of women who'd flirted with the handsome Mr. Harding, fascinated by his looks and mellow American accent. He also recalled how disappointed they'd all ended up.

"Well I'd have been glad to swap places with them. This lady was on the matronly side—she was part of the moral majority on the committee. Once she'd decided that I wasn't about to try to corrupt the city, she insisted I come home for tea, cakes and meeting her daughters. All of them eligible and every one with a face like a barn door, if you get my meaning, Dr. Coppersmith." He nodded to Orlando, who was finding it hard to remain civil to the man, as he was demonstrating an inclination towards flirting with Jonty again.

"And did the lady in question seem determined that you wouldn't escape until marriage had been proposed to one of them?" Jonty spoke lightly although he was well aware of the nervous tension in his voice.

"Well, that's what I thought at first, with all the questions about my family and their business. But then she began to dismiss the young ladies one by one, on errands, until there was just the two of us alone." Jimmy grimaced. "Tell me, have you ever been in a room on your own with a determined woman of nearly fifty? She was almost sitting in my lap before I managed to persuade her to let me go."

"Just how did you manage that?" Jonty was keeping half an eye on the mathematical volcano bubbling up at his side. "I know some very resolute women—my mother is one and the Master of Bride's sister is another. I can't imagine Ariadne Peters letting any man out of her clutches once she'd set her mind on him."

"Oh, I suddenly remembered the old ruse my father had once played when he was being ensnared by an extremely plain but very rich, *old* young lady, if you get my drift. I pleaded that I had to get home as I was a member of a very strict ascetic sect who couldn't be out after dark and had eschewed all the sins of the flesh."

Fortuitously, the waiter arrived to take them into dinner just as Jonty was developing a fit of the giggles.

"Talking of determined women of a certain age, you never met Mama, did you?" Jonty ushered their guest into his seat.

"I've never had that pleasure." Jimmy waited for Orlando to settle before he sat down. Jonty wondered if he were deliberately trying to unsettle him.

"Now there's a woman who might well accost you physically, as some of her unwanted suitors might attest." Nerves made Jonty's tongue run on. "Or people she has affection for. She whacked Orlando just a week ago, for nothing worse than scientific experimentation."

"Then I hope she'll do me the honour of a clip around the ear. You're a lucky man, Coppersmith." If Jimmy hadn't realised what effect his words were having on Orlando, Jonty had. Embarrassment and anger were fighting for mastery on the man's face and in his voice.

Jonty changed the subject to transatlantic travel and the meal went as well as might have been expected, for a while. Orlando tried to remember his manners and not be too antagonistic to Jimmy, as Jonty would no doubt get the hump if he made it too clear he wanted to punch the man. At least he could contribute to a discussion on the virtues of the great liners, and modern transport in general, rather than being made to feel an idiot when they talked about the Bard.

By the time they reached the port and coffee, which they chose to take in the lounge, a superficial degree of mellowness existed among the company, although volcanic emotions still seethed in Orlando's breast.

Fate intervened in the form of an old suitor of Mrs. Stewart's who spotted Jonty, cut him out from his friends, then took him off for a chat regarding the latest doings of the fragrant Helena, which unfortunately left the other two alone.

"You seem very self-assured, Mr. Harding." Orlando had been waiting for his moment to confront this man. With Jonty temporarily occupied, and his spirits emboldened by the wine, he seized the moment.

"I usually feel confident, Dr. Coppersmith. I've been lucky enough in my life to do many things which people have said weren't possible. I rise to a challenge, you might say." Jimmy raised his glass and stared through it, admiring the gentle red colour. "And when I want to do something, I make a point of seeing that I'm successful. I guess that success breeds self-belief."

Cocky swine. Orlando gave the man an icy stare. "Do you achieve everything you want? Doesn't that make life fairly lacklustre?"

"On the contrary, it makes my life a constant delight. And yes, I do tend to get what I want, especially if I want it a lot." He cast his gaze around the dining room, as if looking for something he might take a shine to, let his glance alight on Jonty, linger and then sweep on.

Orlando swallowed hard. There had been an edge to what the man said that chilled him—despite everything that Jonty had averred the day before, he still didn't trust the American as far as he could throw him. Jonty might well be innocent of any untoward interaction with the man, both back in his University

College days and now, but he couldn't think the same of Jimmy. "I can't believe you get everything you want." Orlando snorted, trying to add emphasis, and worried that he just sounded ridiculous.

"Want me to prove it to you?" Jimmy's gimlet gaze, blue eyes piercing into Orlando's, suggested he was throwing down the gauntlet. "I think we both know what I want. Let's see if I can get it." His expression changed to a smile as Jonty rejoined them. "That seemed a pleasant encounter."

"It was. I always enjoy talking to any old friends of Mama, although I'm glad to return to the matter in hand." He tapped the arm of Jimmy's chair. "Now back to the business of this production. Will you wear the kilt or just plaid trousers?"

"Oh the kilt, definitely. It adds enormously to the authenticity of the piece and, of course, the sense of freedom it gives is unbelievable." Jimmy seemed to be playing up his lasciviousness, becoming a caricature of the flirtatious male.

"Are you entitled to wear the tartan, as Dr. Stewart is?" Orlando fixed Jimmy with his gaze—the challenge was ignored.

"Mama forbids the wearing of kilts properly." Jonty restrained a laugh. "We have to put on our underwear, especially at Hogmanay, ever since the time Clarence disgraced himself. You'll remember Clarence?"

"I do." Jimmy grinned. "He gave you that huge bottle of champagne and we all got sloshed."

Orlando didn't like the sound of that at all. This was a story from his lover's past he'd not been made privy to. "Your mother's entirely correct, Jonty. That's the only way for the garment to be worn."

"Nonsense!" Jimmy riposted. "If the old way was good enough for life in the glens then it's more than suitable for Aquae Sulis. I'll be wearing mine in the traditional fashion."

Orlando sneaked a glance at Jonty, who bore a dreamy look, as if he were thinking for a moment of Jimmy in a kilt and it was proving an agreeable vision. "And will the rest of your cast follow suit?"

"Doubt it. They all seem a bit straitlaced to me. I dare say it'll be drawers as usual. Especially Lady Macbeth." Jimmy and his partner in kilt crime giggled while the third man finished his port in stony silence.

Orlando wasn't at all happy with the growing familiarity between these two. "Why have you decided to have a male player for the heroine?"

"Tradition again, Dr. Coppersmith. That's how they did it in Shakespeare's time—it's how he wrote the plays, after all. Some of the jokes don't work if you have women in the parts." Jonty rapped the table.

"It's true. The whole epilogue to *As You Like It* is fairly meaningless and not funny in the least if it's some pretty actress playing Rosalind. With a boy or man it all makes sense." Jimmy's enthusiasm for the Bard was almost as passionate as Jonty's.

"Then you should change the text. Make it work properly."

The fans of Shakespeare looked aghast. "That's like saying you should make one and one come to three if it suits you." Jimmy waggled an admonitory finger. "The text should be sacred, Dr. Coppersmith. Plenty of people have mucked around with it in the past, giving happy endings where none were intended or cutting out the saucier stuff. All sacrilege."

"Jimmy is right, Orlando. It's just about acceptable to cut the longer parts of the text to keep a performance within a certain time, but not to change the essence. Don't you see that?" Jonty wore his most pleading and winning gaze.

"I do not. Sod it and sod the Bard." Orlando rose from the

table, turned on his heels and left, apologising to three old ladies en route for his unnecessary language.

"What's the matter with your friend?" Jimmy broke the long silence, seeming more amused than upset at the scene he'd just seen played out.

Jonty sighed. "He's got a bee in his bonnet. About you." He studied his empty coffee cup, wishing he could find a way to bring this exchange to a swift, civilised end.

"Ah." Jimmy leaned forward so they could talk freely. "Is he more than a friend then?"

Jonty nodded. "We've been very close for the best part of two years. You mustn't tell him I told you."

"You didn't need to, I suspected it from the start. I may not be the most subtle of people—you remember the incident with the chorus girls and the divinity students—but I can read understated signals between people. I need to, it's part of my job to ensure that my actors and actresses convey the most delicate of emotions with a word or a look. Tonight just convinced me that I was right."

Jonty narrowed his eyes. "Just what were you two discussing when I was talking to Lord Tallboy?"

Jimmy grinned again. "I set Orlando a challenge. Or rather I responded to one of his."

"And am I to be enlightened as to the nature of this challenge?"

Jimmy shook his head theatrically. "Oh no, not until I get all my strategy firmly in place. Then you'll know. You'll know very well."

Jonty rose and gestured towards the hotel foyer, his guest reluctantly rising to follow him.

"Hey." Jimmy dawdled, admiring a flower arrangement, a painting. "I've heard of these excellent baths, House of Sulis the place is called. Perhaps you know it?"

Jimmy reopening the conversation just as Jonty was hoping to close it seemed par for the course. Maybe on this occasion he'd reached the crux of what he wished to say. "Orlando and I have been there on a couple of occasions. The baths are truly excellent."

"Perhaps we might visit them together, when Dr. Coppersmith is busy with his texts? You must get bored."

"N-no," Jonty stammered. Such a direct approach surprised him, unless he was reading too much into an innocent invitation to bathe. Maybe he was doing his old friend an injustice. "Sorry, what I mean is that in addition to finishing my paper, we have a commission—a case to investigate—and we'll need all our spare time to do so."

"Does that mean you can't help with the play?" Jimmy looked disappointed, but whether about the Bard or the baths he didn't make clear.

"Of course not, although I think I'll have to pass up the chance of doing some acting. I'm sorry."

"Not a problem. As long as we can pick your brains we can find plenty of people to impersonate a tree or swing a *claidheamh mòr*." Jimmy held out his hand to shake. "Perhaps you'll clear up that mystery and we can take that dip together one day."

"Indeed." Jonty shook the man's hand and watched him depart. One tricky situation had been dealt with—now another had to be tackled. He sighed and began to climb the stairs.

Chapter Five

Orlando paced around his room, fuming. *You let yourself down again, acting like a petulant little boy and having tantrums.* Jonty had done nothing to deserve his wrath even if Mr. Smarmy Pants had. Remembering Jimmy, Orlando's sense of outrage overcame the guilt for a while; he'd been challenged directly, not in as many words but the intent was plain. The man was out to steal Jonty from him, that much was obvious, and it just wasn't cricket. Orlando swung a kick at the fire dogs, immediately regretting the action when he whacked his toe.

He wished this annoying American with the smooth voice and cocky face was some effeminate creature, all simpering and mincing gait, the sort of chap Jonty couldn't stand. Jonty had once been invited to a reception for a theatrical company who put on a show at the university's Amateur Dramatic Club, and he'd dragged his lover along, expecting the affair to be great fun. A preponderance of effeminate men in attendance had danced about the pair, fawning and making strange comments. Jonty, normally at ease in all company from royalty down to barrow boys, had been uncomfortable and unhappy. He'd confessed afterwards that the men had reminded him of Timothy Taylor, which had been enough to fill Orlando with loathing. Taylor had been one of the boys who'd abused Jonty at school and had grown into an epicene, prematurely aged figure.

Anyway, Jonty had always liked "real" men, masculinity being a trait he prized almost above all others. As he put it, *if I'd wanted to kiss a woman, I'd have found the real thing and not some poor substitute.*

Which was exactly why Orlando felt so uneasy about his potential rival. He produced the occasional act of flamboyance or outlandish remark, but generally the man reeked of masculinity. Worse still, he was just the type whom Jonty fancied, like Richard Marsters had been and Orlando himself was. Tall, dark-haired, slim. All that Jimmy lacked was the intellectual severity.

Matthew Ainslie was built on the same lines. The previous summer, once Orlando had got over the enormous shock that the man seemed to fancy *him*, he'd become convinced that Jonty had wanted to get to know Ainslie better, and it had earned him a punch. His jealousy had been illogical, he knew, and even when Jonty constantly reassured him he had eyes for no one else, Orlando still found it hard to believe. A little nagging voice in his cerebral cortex kept telling him Jonty would be bound to leave if he found a more worthy companion. Those same doubts were re-surfacing now.

Orlando could see the pair of men in his mind's eye. They'd be down in the lounge, laughing, discussing Shakespeare in a way which he and Jonty never could. Jimmy would have a predatory eye on the golden-haired creature sitting beside him and a sneer on his face—he was sure that the look would be a sneer—for *his* rightful companion.

Orlando tortured himself over and again with these thoughts, not seeing a word or equation on the pages of the book he'd picked up to distract himself with. Part of him wanted to go downstairs, all smiles and confidence, and cut Jonty out from under Mr. Fancy Pants's nose, showing him effectively who was boss. Part of him was too ashamed to face Jonty again, having been reassured so recently that the man had never, would never, be unfaithful. The other part simply wanted to punch Jimmy on the nose and have done with.

Orlando sat deep in his thoughts, eyes scanning the pages of his book yet seeing nothing, ears not registering the very slight noise the door made as it swept over the carpet nor the cat-like tread of stockinged feet as they made their way up behind him.

His first inklings of the mischief afoot were the strong arms which enfolded him—making him leap a good six inches in the air—and the little nose that snuggled into his shoulders, probably having had his neck as its target but being foiled by the jolt.

And the voice which said, "Orlando, don't be such an idiot. It doesn't become you."

"I'm not an idiot. Well, not this time." Orlando nestled his head backwards onto his lover's.

"You shouldn't let Jimmy get to you like this. It's just his way, typical of some of those brash Americans."

"Rex Prefontaine wasn't brash." Orlando twisted his lover round, making him sit next to him on the settee. "He was civilised, witty and self effacing."

"I didn't say all of our ex-colonial friends are like that, just a few, and Jimmy's one of them. He used to delight in winding up the more pompous members of University College. Got himself punched once or twice, and I actually think he rather enjoyed it." Jonty rose, drawing Orlando up with him. "You need some fresh air. We'll take a stroll down to the river—it'll raise your spirits. And no 'buts'. Dr. Stewart insists."

Orlando didn't speak until they were on the towpath by the river. "He challenged me. Just like being called out in the olden days." The walk seemed to be having a calming effect on him, the combined magic of star and moonlight working its spell. It couldn't, however, seem to clear his mind of a certain person. "He said—not in so many words, but there was plenty implied— that he was going to make a beeline for you. That he was used to getting what he wanted and that he had his eye on your rather nice little frame." Orlando beat some railings as vehemently as if they were Jimmy's face.

"Oh, did he? I don't doubt it. He—" Jonty was about to add *made a bit of a pass at me* but decided that would only make the situation much worse. He quickly changed his thread, "—always was a cocky so and so. Well this is one challenge he won't succeed with. I said I was yours alone and I mean it." He tapped Orlando's cheek affectionately, the nearest they'd ever get to a kiss in public. "Now, we have to get a plan together for this case we've taken on. I don't suppose there's any chance we could detect together in the morning and work in the afternoon?" They did need to sort out the logistics and the process would effectively distract Orlando from the matter of *you know who* for a moment as they ambled back to the Grand.

"I'd love to do that, Jonty, but it just wouldn't work out. The time I can get at those books on my own, without being interrupted by other readers milling around, is strictly in the morning. Those books aren't the only ones being sold off and sometimes I think half the academics in Britain are up here looking for a bargain. And your acting crowd don't get up till after noon, do they?"

Jonty was relieved to see, at long last, a vestige of a smile on his lover's face. "I think they might when the wind's in the right direction, but rehearsals are strictly scheduled for afternoon and evening. We'll just have to work separately then try to team up on Sundays when we're both free. At least that should let us cover twice the ground. If the worst came to the worst we could stay on a few more days, I'm sure. Or one of us could."

Orlando considered. "You need to get back to Cambridge—you can't swing the lead with that book more than the stipulated time. I suspect you've hardly anything left to do on it."

"It's mostly done, just lacking one vital thing to give it punch and I've got that buzzing about in the back of my head like a fly which won't settle to be swatted. All the rest is almost ready to be typed up and I've found a bureau here to do it, once I've cracked that last little bit."

"Sounds like a re-run of the Woodville Ward." Orlando grinned. "There's not a murder mystery hidden away in those sonnets of yours, is there?"

"No, just a plain old affair of the heart. It's a matter of jealousy and that's something I find quite hard to get my noddle around. I can spout the official line on *Othello* till the cows come home but I don't feel it in here." Jonty thumped his chest dramatically, immediately regretting that he'd made reference to the green-eyed monster when he saw how discomforted Orlando appeared. They walked on in silence.

"Anyway, I thought you were the university expert on the sonnets?"

"Yes." The hotel foyer had almost emptied now, the doorkeeper seemingly grateful for someone to attend to. Jonty slipped the man sixpence, a rather-tinged-with-guilt sixpence. "The early ones, yes. I can get my teeth into those without any trouble at all, although they're a totally different kettle of fish. Do you know that they were bowdlerised for years, Orlando? All the references to a man cut out and a lady put in? I'm only just getting it into the noddle of some of my colleagues, let alone the dunderheads, that our dear Will S. was besotted by some handsome man as well as by his dark lady."

"At least maths doesn't carry quite those complications." Orlando opened the door to their suite in a cautious manner.

Jonty wondered if he expected Jimmy to pop out from the escritoire. He pointed towards the desk where his manuscript lay. "If this is a success, then I'll write a similar one about the master-mistress poetry, and pretty hot stuff it'll be, before they cut all the juicy bits out at the printer's." He tapped his friend's arm. "Now, if you wish to give me fresh inspiration for that tome, then you'd better be getting about it." He raised his hand to gently draw it down his lover's face.

Orlando turned his face to kiss the hand which caressed him. "*Thy sweet love remembered such wealth brings.*"

"That's the stuff. I'll knock all the numbers out of you yet." Jonty leaned in for a kiss, stole two, then took his lover's hand. "*And so to bed*, to change authors in mid conversation."

"One day you'll find that you've used up your entire lifetime's worth of conversation. I'll have a bit of peace and quiet for once and you'll have to write everything down." Orlando kissed his lover ardently. "Now be hushed for once and just let me love you as I crave."

Jonty pulled his lover's hand up into the moonlight that pierced the clouds, then traced his finger across the palm.

"What are you up to now?"

"Practicing for when I lose my power of speech, or—as now—am ordered to silence." Jonty drew his hand across his mouth as though sealing it, then, pressing his index finger back on Orlando's palm, formed clearly the words *As you wish,* over again as he was manoeuvred towards the bedroom.

"I think I could get used to you being quiet." Orlando got to work on his lover's buttons, always keen to have bare flesh under his fingers. For reasons as yet unclear to Jonty, Orlando hated to make love, *do his duty,* with either of them in partial dress. Maybe it was yet another undiscovered legacy from his bleak childhood years.

They played their usual parts in the prologue, the scene-setting for the drama to unfold in his chamber, where the main prop would be a double bed, and only two actors necessary to the performance. Jonty gently stripped Orlando's jacket, shirt and tie, interspersing the dresser's role with tender kisses or fierce, as the occasion demanded. The skin beneath was milk-white, like a maiden's in some depiction of St. George, although the forearms were like Bath Stone, testament to the hours they'd spent in their garden, shirtsleeves rolled up as they sweated over shrubs or tree roots.

"I take that back." Orlando broke off from a particularly succulent kiss. "I don't like it at all when you're quiet—it's completely unnerving. What are you thinking about?"

"Actually, I was thinking about that patch we cleared at the bottom of the garden..."

"Why did I ever think you romantic? Just as well you weren't the Bard's rival poet, you'd have eclipsed him ten times over with your *patch at the bottom of the garden.* What happened to *in fresh numbers number all your graces?*"

"I seem to recall—" Jonty insinuated his fingers into Orlando's waistband, "—promising to knock all the numbers out of your head, or at least—" the fingers wriggled closer to their target, "—stroke them out. Or something."

"I think that *something* would be more than acceptable." Orlando's voice, hoarse and husky, suggested he could barely think. He eased Jonty back, tipping him onto the bed in a gesture that was no doubt supposed to be manly and brutal, but which, in reality, was tender and thoughtful.

Poor Orlando, so trusting, so kind. Jonty couldn't help but

shiver with guilt at the thoughts he'd been having about Jimmy, hoping that his lover would interpret the trembling as excitement. "*Something* it is, then. The usual something or something a bit different?"

"If you say that word once more it'll sound meaningless." Orlando was trembling now, with what could only be anticipation. "What was the bit different you had in mind?"

"Well, the usual, actually. Just turnabout, sort of." Jonty felt as if he'd lost all connection between brain and tongue, embarrassed beyond reason to speak plainly of things which he would unhesitatingly *do* with his lover.

"Oh." Orlando didn't need to say any more. He clearly wasn't ready for such a departure from his usual role—Jonty might have been ready (in body if not in words) to reverse the characters, but he'd forgotten how much his friend disliked change. Far too much of the old Coppersmith was still present.

"Then it'll be the usual, then." Jonty tried to keep the disappointment from his voice. One day it would happen, he'd just have to be patient. And the guilt he already felt over Jimmy Harding would save him from wanting to press the matter.

"Ah." Orlando drew his lover close, both the relief in his voice and the strength in his arms emphasising how much happier he was now. It only took a few minutes for any lingering sense of disappointment to begin to clear—he might be wary of innovation, he might be tentative, at times he could be forceful, but Orlando Coppersmith was a magnificent lover. Now, in just his pants and in the half light of the moon through the gap in the curtains, he resembled some Greek god, bestowing his favours on a lucky human.

Soon Jonty felt alive all over, tingling and burning, wishing for hands to move lower, only not too soon. Such were the frustrations of lovemaking, the desire for things to move on, to accelerate, reach their natural end, tempered against the enjoyment of the moment, the languid sensuality that savoured the simpler, more innocent kisses and caresses.

"Is that nice?" Orlando was addressing a spot just below Jonty's collarbone, having his lover pinned—not too firmly—to the mattress.

"Oh, yes. Wonderful." Jonty sighed, the tingling sensations in his backbone proving both pleasurable and distracting. "How about this?" He inched his fingers down to the place which drove Orlando mad when it was stroked, gently, for minutes on end.

"Ah."

There was no more talk for a while. Only moans, murmurs, tiny incoherent whispers which might just have contained the words *I love you* or maybe *I'm so close.* The sweet, tender coupling, the predestined end to all the kisses and caresses, came as naturally as breathing, no longer any matter of awkwardness or discomfort, bodies so used to one another, so ready to accommodate and be accommodated.

"Thank you," Orlando whispered against his lover's neck, body still trembling.

"No need to thank me." Jonty held Orlando close, strong arms protecting, hands touching familiar skin. "Come on, we both need a bit of sleep."

He didn't dare ask why his lover should suddenly want to voice his gratitude for lovemaking—he had an awful feeling he could put a name to the answer.

📖

Mrs. Morgan, she of the nodding terms with Dr. Keane, wasn't as Jonty expected her to be, although he wasn't sure what he had in mind for a retired whore. He'd met two of the king's old mistresses over the years; one had been very haughty and full of herself, struggling to maintain her beauty against all odds, the other had let herself slide gracefully into a mellow middle age and was very jolly, still proving good company. This woman seemed tired and plain with no hint in her of what men had once found so attractive. Perhaps there had never been anything in particular, just her availability and a willingness to do whatever was required, for a small fee.

Jonty had found her easily enough—she was cleaning the bar at the little pub which, according to their informant, she jointly ran with Mr. Morgan. Keane had given them clear directions about finding the tavern down by the canal, and when Jonty had mentioned that gentleman's name to the landlady, it had been introduction enough.

He hadn't beat about the bush, he hadn't got the time for that, raising the matter of Sarah Carter straight away and simply asking if Mrs. Morgan had any light to shed on the matter.

The woman shrugged. "That's none of my business—too long ago now for any of us to do anything about it. And why should such a gentleman as you be taking an interest after all this time?"

Jonty felt, not for the first occasion in his investigating career, that he was the one being interrogated.

"I have a commission from the son of Dr. Buckner. He's fulfilling his father's dying wish that the girl's death be properly looked into." Jonty hoped to play on the woman's sentimentality, if she had any. "I know there's little hope of finding anything afresh at such a remove, but I did hope a person of decency and common sense—" he smiled at Mrs. Morgan, implying she was certainly that, "—would be able to

71

assist me. Is there nothing you can tell me of Miss Carter herself?"

The woman produced a sly smile. "She wasn't a Miss. You're wrong on that to start with." She carried on wiping the bar counter. "I've work to do here and only me to do it unless I pay the girl for an extra hour and I can't afford to be doing that."

"If you tell me the truth, I'll pay the girl's extra hour myself, now." Jonty reached in his jacket for his wallet. "Then she can make us both some tea which I'll recompense you for, and well over the odds." He fixed her with a steely glare. "However, if I find I've been paying for lies and flummery then I'll make sure the magistrate takes Mr. Morgan's licence away."

He smiled enigmatically, in part because it was an idle threat and he hadn't the first idea of how to get a licence to sell alcohol revoked, but on this occasion his bluff wasn't called. The girl was, meaning Jonty and his hostess were soon drinking something which passed for tea and discussing the dead woman.

"So, did you ever meet Mr. Carter?"

Mrs. Morgan shook her head. "He'd supposedly gone off somewhere when Sarah was still living back in Bristol. Not that I knew her well, you know, but when she died there was a lot of gossip and it all came out."

"She didn't wear her wedding ring?"

"Not that I ever saw. And I'd have noticed."

Jonty could believe it—whatever else this woman was, she wasn't dull-witted. "And was there any gossip about *him*?"

"I heard he was a sailor, girl in every port and she was the one for Bristol. He's probably off at the Cape with some brown doxy now." Mrs. Morgan sipped her tea then drew her finger around the rim of the cup. "I suppose you think we were the lowest of the low, but we didn't need to look too far for business. Plenty of very fine gentlemen would pay us in those days, not just Dr. Keane. Two groups of folk were using the baths that night. Our group, that was me and—I can't remember the girl's name, she moved to London not long afterwards—and our gentlemen. Sarah Carter was with the other crowd and they was said to be the real gentry. There was another girl or two used to hang around with her. They were both there that night although I never knew their names."

"What was there about Mrs. Carter that made her so popular, do you think? Was she a beauty?"

"No, not really. One of the girls who hung around with her was, you'd call her a real stunner, yet Sarah was the one the men used to like. She made them laugh, I suppose, the really pretty one was always too po-faced to do that. When we were both at the baths together, our two groups of gentlemen, the others were always smiling and joking, much more than we ever did." She stared out of the window, as if she were hoping to catch a glimpse of the girl she'd been twenty-five years since.

"Did you ever suspect that there had been foul play?"

"No. They said that it was her heart and we all believed it. We were all shocked, our gentlemen as well, and it rather took the shine off things for a while. That and not being able to go back to the baths. That had become a special place for us all, so after we were banned from there it all sort of fizzled out. There were no more parties, just the usual and that increasingly rarely..."

Jonty could guess what *the usual* might have been, from tales his father had told of his less upright friends and their boating trips down to Skindles. "Have you any idea who might have left flowers on her grave, or who might still do so?"

"No idea at all. I've not thought of Sarah Carter for years, not even out of curiosity."

Jonty, accepting he had no more to be gained, pushed his tea away largely undrunk then left the pub, walking along the towpath towards the city and mulling over the little he'd learned. He decided to try to make a second call that morning, to another lady who had once been of ill repute. Dr. Buckner had obtained names (of a sort) for three of the four other prostitutes who'd been present the night of the murder. Mrs. Morgan was one and her companion had been known as 'Roulette'. The now-respectable woman at the inn hadn't been able to translate that alias into something usable. The other name Jonty had on his list was Clarissa Simmonds, and while Dr. Buckner senior had given a place where she might have been found in the 1880s, he hadn't given an address for more recent times. Nor had Keane any information to give, as this girl had been with the other group.

Undaunted, Jonty decided to begin at the original location. Plenty of people could still be found in the same house they'd lived in a quarter of a century ago, although Clarissa wasn't one of them. A harassed housewife with an infant at her skirts opened the door to him, was shocked at meeting such a well-dressed and well-spoken gentleman at her step then swore that she'd no knowledge of any one called Simmonds ever having lived there.

Jonty thanked her and was turning away when he was recalled with a coarse cry. "Old Mrs. Franklin might know. She's lived around here since Noah came out of the ark."

"And where can I find this antediluvian lady?" Jonty grinned.

The housewife stood a little taller, preening herself a bit, which seemed to be the normal reaction in women whom Jonty had to deal with. He hoped they weren't trying to impress him.

"She lives on the next floor up." The woman indicated the flight of stairs behind her, leading up into the gloom of a house which had fallen into disrepair. "I can take you there."

"There's no need—I'll call if I get lost." Jonty thrust a two-bob piece into the woman's hand then set off up the stairs, hoping he didn't get lost as he wasn't enamoured of the predatory look forming in her eye.

Two doors opened from the landing—he mentally tossed a coin and knocked at the one to his left. A voice informed him that someone was coming and the door was eventually opened by a neat, sprightly old lady with white hair and a bright smile, one that grew wider as she appraised her visitor.

"Mrs. Franklin?" Jonty was pleased to see that this lady was four times as clean as the one who'd met him on the step. The little glance he had of the room behind her spoke of neatness and order.

"That's me. Can I help you?"

"If you can tell me anything about Clarissa Simmonds, then you certainly can."

"I can..." The lady hesitated. "But why anyone should be asking about poor Clarissa after all these years... Still, you'd better come in. I've just made a pot of tea. Would you like a cup?"

Jonty recalled the awful brew he'd been offered at the pub, was about to refuse then remembered his manners and agreed. He was delighted and amazed to find that it really was a refreshing concoction, one he sipped with relish.

"Now, what do you want to know?" Mrs. Franklin settled into a chair, obviously a favourite one given the sagging nature of a seat which enfolded her frame perfectly.

"Anything at all." Jonty told the story of the House of Sulis, of Buckner's desire to see someone brought to book, of

75

Clarissa's being one of the names mentioned.

Mrs. Franklin listened with much evidence of a keen mind, asking a question here or there to get things entirely clear. When the account was finished, she nodded her head, offered Jonty a biscuit and then began her own report. "I'm afraid you're just a bit too late, dear. If you'd come here as a boy of—" she considered him for a moment, "—let's say fifteen, then you might have seen her. She died the winter of 1895, it was the consumption, you know."

Jonty nodded—he understood. Every time tuberculosis was mentioned he thought of his first love, Richard Marsters, and it still pained him.

"I know she was what your mother might call a fallen woman."

Jonty grinned at the appropriateness of the term—Mrs. Stewart used it often regarding her charitable work.

"But she was kind to me. I had been ill the previous summer and she'd fetched and carried, so when she was poorly I was able to return the compliment as best I could. I had been a nurse once, before I was married. She was a nice girl."

"I don't doubt it. Did she ever mention Sarah Carter?"

"Not by name, I think. Although she did talk—when she knew the end was near, you know—about that night at the baths. She said that a girl had died and it had all been covered up. I asked her if she wanted me to fetch a policeman so she could tell him, but she said it had been too long before, 'and if no one had been interested then, they weren't likely to be now, were they?' It's a shame she didn't live to meet you." Mrs. Franklin smiled, instantly reminding Jonty of his beloved grandmother.

"Did she say anything I might find of use?"

"Only that she didn't believe the death was due to heart

failure, although that's not news to you, is it? Let me think. She said the girl was supposed to have a husband somewhere or t'other, but she was certain he'd not been there that night. 'Not getting revenge for what his wife was up to.' Yes, that's right— she said exactly that and then she laughed, a bit funny you might say. What's the word? Ruefully. She said that Sarah had told her it was a shame she was already wed, as she had a man who was paying attention. She wasn't interested in divorce or bigamy, so that was the end of that."

"Did Clarissa say who the man was?"

"No. I'm not sure she knew. Not one of the usual clients, I'd have thought—they were far too high and mighty to be thinking of taking her down the aisle. Mind you, I could be wrong. This is all third-hand stuff."

"And there's nothing else you could tell me? You've been very helpful so far."

"Nonsense. It's been my pleasure to entertain a handsome young man. Especially as I bet *her downstairs* has been jealous of me." A wicked grin crossed Mrs. Franklin's face. "I'm sounding like Clarissa now. She was a great one for the gentlemen, even up to the end." She frowned. "Now that's something might be of use. She had a man used to visit her, one she said she'd known right back to her young days. He's still living in Bath—I see him down by the Abbey sometimes. Mr. Bredon his name is, he lives on Pulteney Street. I wonder if he'd be able to help. He was very upset when Clarissa died. Sent a lovely bunch of lilies to her funeral."

"Did he? I must meet him to find out where he got them." Jonty smiled and Mrs. Franklin blushed like a giddy girl again.

Chapter Six

Orlando was in a foul mood. Friday had started badly and had grown worse as it progressed. No, that was inaccurate. It could never be described as an inauspicious start when the first words you heard were, "Hello Orlando, lovely to see you," and then found a sleepy, satiated Jonty Stewart at your side. He decided he really should count his blessings before he began to enumerate his woes.

The misery had started when Orlando had turned up at the private library where the manuscripts and books were stored, to find it locked. It was a good fifty minutes later, during which various other people had turned up, gone off to enquire then returned none the wiser, that a flustered gentleman had arrived with a huge bunch of keys. He'd explained, rather slowly as if he were talking to five-year-olds, that the usual custodian had been taken ill and that he'd come to open up for them, assuming he could work out which of the keys on his bunch was the correct one.

In what seemed like a fortnight, the man at last had the doors opened and Orlando was able to make a beeline for his morning's work. He'd found two badly water-stained books, handwritten in a tiny, almost cryptic hand, which he'd been assured contained wondrous mathematical treasures. Neither was so badly damaged as to be condemned out of hand and so they both had to be pored through to find out whether there were nuggets of knowledge lurking in their pages or whether they weren't worth the parchment they were written on. Fond memories of the Woodville Ward case, of his own amnesia and the glorious second wooing of Jonty, flooded through Orlando's mind as he enjoyed the feel of the old material under his fingers.

This proved his only satisfaction of the morning, though. The first book seemed interesting enough but the damage to the middle part of it made it impossible to follow the theorem adequately and the last few pages seemed to have been cut out with a knife. Cursing himself for not doing Jonty's trick of looking at the end of the book first, Orlando set about the second tome, the one the custodian had particularly praised. This seemed much more hopeful, beginning with an intriguing proposition that was developed, or at least seemed to be, over the succeeding pages, what he could make out of them. The middle part was missing again, but at least the end seemed to be all present, and Orlando became excited about the theorem being explored.

The other occupants of the library had a terrible shock as a loud *harrumph* rent the air. Orlando had found the wonderful hypothesis fizzled out into a load of pretentious nonsense, full of leaps of logic and impossible assumptions which made no sense. From being a treasure trove, this had turned out to be shoddy and reprehensible scholarship of the very worst kind. The university wouldn't pay tuppence for such slovenly work— they got plenty of that for free from the dunderheads.

An entirely fruitless morning then, followed by a lunch of sandwiches taken in his room, Jonty having gone off to see the actors up on the hill and taking a cheese roll with them, no doubt. That was another source of annoyance. Their conversation over breakfast had concerned jealousy and Jonty's inability to empathise with the emotion.

"And that's the problem with this dark lady woman, is it? You can't understand how Old Will gets into such a state about her?" Orlando hadn't particularly wanted the Bard over his sausages, but if Jonty got a bee in his bonnet, you couldn't shift it.

"I know what Shakespeare's saying, yet I can't put myself in his place and really get to the heart of things. How can I prepare my nice little idiots' guide to the sonnets—which will launch my publishing career and no doubt become a standard work for all undergraduates of taste and intelligence—if I can't get this burning covetousness and sense of unworthiness into the thing? I mean in more than just an objective manner? Couldn't you go and get yourself a nice little missy to chase after you and make the green-eyed monster rise in my breast?"

The remark had made Orlando snort. If Jonty wanted to know about jealousy he should come and change places with *him* for a few days. Then there'd be no problem in experiencing envy, or feeling lack of worth. He'd pointedly changed the subject to trigonometry.

Orlando took as long as he could over his lunch, well aware that he should be going out talking to people in relation to the investigation. He didn't feel like talking to anybody, except one, of course. He'd be quite happy to go and tell a certain Mr. Harding a few home truths. He even had a few choice words in mind, *leave off, my fist* and *your nose* being among the more repeatable ones.

He decided he needed comfort and as his main source of it wasn't present he determined to take refuge among boxes, lists, arrows and underlinings. Producing paper and his favourite pen, he began to make a list of the people they knew to have been present the night of the murder alongside any information he had about them.

Five women were listed. Mary Maguire, now Mary Morgan, and the girl with the nickname Roulette had both been with Dr Keane's party. The other three had associated with the second group of men—the dead girl, Clarissa Simmonds and another for whom not even a pet name was known. They had an address only for Mary Morgan. Orlando considered the list, wondering whether Jonty had achieved anything during the morning; hopefully more success than he'd encountered.

The list of men provided a similar group of the known and unknown, dead and alive. There had been four of them with Dr. Keane, including one person so far unidentified. These had been confirmed by Keane himself, who'd also provided up-to-date addresses for two of the men. He hadn't been able to provide a name for the unknown man, assuring Orlando that he'd been an acquaintance of a chap called Patterson, brought along for the first time that night and never seen again, something which seemed suspicious in light of a suspected murder.

The logical thing would have been to talk to Patterson about this friend who'd disappeared so spectacularly, but that wasn't possible. He'd died of dysentery in Peshawar ten years previously and had probably taken his friend's identity to the grave with him. While Orlando found this unbelievably frustrating, fond as he was of dotting all the i's and crossing all the t's, he'd already agreed with Jonty that they would, at least for the time being, concern themselves only with the other group of men, the ones who'd been with Sarah Carter.

They hadn't yet confirmed the identity of any in this second group, only having Buckner's word for the five of them. The Honourable (why were there so many of those about?) Jeremy Weir (now deceased), Mr. Bredon (whom Orlando had tried in vain to see), Thomas Critchley, Phillip Gibbs and, again, a person unknown. Buckner's more recent notes listed addresses for Gibbs and they'd already decided that Jonty should be chasing up Thomas Critchley, as the man had been an old flame of his mother's. Richard Stewart would be able to rouse out an address for him.

Orlando scribbled down some other ideas—florists, undertakers, cleaning ladies—a whole stream of folk who might have something to add to the story. For the first time in his investigating career he appreciated what a lot of sheer, boring legwork might be involved in a case. They'd been lucky so far that only one of their investigations had involved a lot of running about, and then they'd had the assistance of a marvellous solicitor whose men had done most of it. Orlando wished he had those minions here now.

They would just have to concentrate their resources, trying to follow up leads as they came, although Orlando had a horrible feeling at the back of his mind that they simply might not solve this case in the time available, if ever. He supposed they could always come back to Bath and try to get to the bottom of the case on a later occasion—it wasn't as if anyone else would be at risk from this killer, unless the investigation should show up more murders. Still, they'd cracked a mystery that was hundreds of years old. What was a quarter of a century compared to that?

He put down his pen and sighed; for all that he'd wanted a new case to dabble in, a profound sense of dissatisfaction hung about him. He felt a horrible, perplexing fear that this would be their first failure and had no idea what he was supposed to do next. Probably that blasted Jimmy Harding and his challenge was nagging away at the back of Orlando's bonce and making it impossible to think clearly. He muttered to himself in imitation of his lover, who rather liked the expression, *what can't be cured must be endured*, then set off to find Phillip Gibbs.

The Royal Crescent wasn't the only place in Bath with magnificent houses. It had a many a lesser imitation and in one of these Phillip Gibbs lived with his family, according to Buckner's notes. Orlando set off to find the place, choosing foot over cab as it would give him time to think through his strategy. It would hardly be the easiest thing to step into a man's home and accuse him of being involved in the killing of a lady of ill repute.

The decision to walk turned out to be an enormously fortunate one—as Orlando strode up a road lined with offices and shops, he passed one with a shining brass plate that announced its occupants as solicitors. Idly glancing at it and striding on, he immediately retraced his steps. A name had penetrated into his subconscious even if he hadn't knowingly registered it; these were the offices of a Mr. P. Gibbs, a Mr. A. Gibbs and a Mr. H. Cattermole. He knew from Buckner's notes that his quarry had entered the legal profession, so it would be worth a try here. At least within a solicitor's office a conversation could be held confidentially, and that would suit Orlando down to the ground.

He opened the door and introduced himself to the clerk, giving the man the benefit of his full credentials and asking whether it would be possible to see Mr. *P.* Gibbs. He was informed that if he would wait awhile then Mr. Gibbs would have finished with his present client and might be able to give Dr. Coppersmith some moments of his time. Orlando wondered, with a shudder, whether this clerk had read the by-now-infamous *Times* article in which Richard Stewart had sung the praises of the detecting skills of his son and his friend. It had given the men a certain notoriety and definitely opened a door or two but in terms of retaining any degree of subterfuge it was becoming a distinct liability.

Gibbs soon emerged, saw his previous client off with the

right amount of charm and professional unction, then nodded his head slightly in Orlando's direction. The clerk drew him to one side, explained the situation and soon Orlando was inside Gibbs's office, taking a deep breath. He'd decided, as he waited, that there was no point in prevaricating or working slowly up to his point. Better to simply state his commission and seek for information as objectively as possible. With, of course, a keen eye for whether he thought the man was lying or being obstructive.

Gibbs seemed amiable and, on the face of it, willing to help as much as he could. Yes, he remembered the night in question—he wasn't proud of the time he had spent at the House of Sulis, but that had been when he was young and more than willing to sow his wild oats. "I've been married this last fifteen years and my wife is completely understanding of my rather boisterous past, having three brothers herself."

Orlando decided that Bath must be peopled with men to whom he took instant dislike. He tried to concentrate on the facts. "Do you remember Sarah Carter?"

"I do, although one of the other girls, Clarissa, was my *special friend.* As for the other men present, I'm afraid I knew no one in the other party. I still keep in touch with Bredon— play bridge with him quite regularly. I've not seen Thomas Critchley this past twenty years." Gibbs counted the names off on his fingers. "Jeremy Weir is dead, although his mother still lives in Bath, and the fifth man was a friend of Bredon's and I'm not sure of his name. Appleton, possibly. I think he might have travelled abroad."

Orlando pressed the solicitor on the matter of the night itself, whether he had any memory of the order of events, something which Buckner's diaries signally omitted to mention.

Gibbs thought for a moment. After checking that the door

was completely closed, he sat again, leaning forward confidentially. "I shall be entirely frank, or as much as I can at this remove, the events having become rather blurred in my memory. We had all been in the main bath, although at times various pairings had used some of the smaller rooms, returning to the main baths to rest and refresh themselves. Pairs of us paid more visits to the private rooms, I don't need to specify why, then the cat was set among the pigeons. Doctor Buckner swept in like an avenging angel and cleared the temple of its filth—his words, not mine, Dr. Coppersmith. We all dressed hurriedly and went off into the night."

"You didn't see Sarah Carter after the second occasion when you'd all met in the main bath?"

"As far as I'm aware, no."

"And did you see anyone linger after the others had gone?"

"Again, no. Although we were all too keen to be getting ourselves home to be taking a great interest in other people's doings. I heard of the death some days afterwards, when an inquest was held, but I never thought to enquire further."

As the man spoke, Orlando's mind began to dwell on the sordid nature of the events which the solicitor's smooth, objective account sought to hide in professional language. It made him feel physically sick, as always happened when he contemplated sexual activity that wasn't within the context of a loving relationship. Bodies bought and sold like meat, pleasure and intimacy shared for the exchange of coin, simply scandalised him. He could never do such things; neither could his Jonty, or so he assured himself, perhaps a little too vehemently. He even began to wonder whether he'd be able to return to the House of Sulis and enjoy taking the waters as they had over the last few days. Somehow the innocent beauty of the place was becoming soiled.

There seemed little else to be gained from the conversation, so Orlando got Gibbs's agreement that he could return if he felt a further interview was needed, then asked Gibbs to let him know if he thought of anything in the interim. He had little hopes on that score—he'd exacted the promise from many an interviewee but rarely had they come back to him.

Locating Jeremy Weir's mother seemed a logical prospect, so Orlando set off for the police station where he was determined to play the *friend of Inspector Wilson* card for all it was worth. The strategy worked perfectly, especially as the young constable at the desk was someone who'd come across the names Coppersmith and Stewart in connection with the solution of mysteries. Perhaps there were some advantages to this notoriety.

They appealed to the sergeant, who was delighted to be helping out such a noted detective, although his allusion to Sherlock Holmes wasn't welcomed by Orlando, try as he might to hide the fact. Comparisons to that old curmudgeon were wearing a bit thin. The policemen had, however, been able to provide an address for Mrs. Weir, who turned out to be the dowager Duchess of Castle Combe, a lady who'd eschewed the lodge on her elder son's estate for an elegant house on the Crescent. They also confided, in strictest confidence, that they'd been in contact with the lady not a year back about the matter of some missing jewellery, which had been eventually traced to a member of her staff.

As Orlando set off, address in hand, he reflected on how the investigations he and Jonty undertook never seemed to be simple. One thing would lead off on a tangent and there would be no end of paths to follow before a conclusion was reached, like a maze in which one had to explore every dead end, just in case, before the centre could be reached. It was so easy to leap at any new fact—an unknown man, a robbery—and assume that it must be connected to the case in hand. The answer could turn out to be devastatingly simple once the whole story was known.

He consulted his little map to decide the best way to the Duchess's house, whether cab or Shank's pony, made a resolution in favour of the former and set off for the rank. En route he spotted a florist's shop and was immediately struck by the beautiful display of lilies in the window. A sign boldly proclaimed that this was the only place in Bath where such exotic specimens could be obtained. Memories of Jonty's story about Sarah Carter's grave came flooding back so he stepped inside the door.

Orlando had once spent a happy half hour talking to the head gardener down at the Old Manor about the matter of hothouse blooms, so could employ all that he'd learned then to enter into a knowledgeable conversation with the lady behind the counter about the variety of flowers which graced her window. He then turned to their likely provenance, the difficulties of keeping such glorious things in a decent condition and the particular problems in obtaining them all the year around as some fine ladies demanded, wanting Easter flowers to grace their Christmas tables.

Miss Roberts and her assistant Miss Allen (Orlando was amazed at how quickly they gave their names) seemed happy to discuss lilies or orchids with him until the cows came home, or at least until the shop shut, but time pressed on and he needed to make some progress.

"So this is the only place in Bath I can buy such exotics?"

"Oh yes. The only other supply would be the glasshouses of private homes. And they wouldn't sell to anyone, even if he were a gentleman like yourself." Miss Roberts simpered.

"I wonder, then—" Orlando was pleased with the airy sound

of his voice, "—if you would be able to provide a floral tribute for my aunt's grave." Visions of having to explain to Jonty why a lily wreath had suddenly appeared in their hotel room were quickly put aside.

"We'd happily take such a commission. We're used to providing flowers for funerals—hothouse arrangements are very popular."

"Perhaps I might just purchase a small arrangement so I can show my uncle an example before I take a more ostentatious display?"

Miss Allen set to with alacrity, weaving stems and creating a small work of art, one which Orlando felt he could get away with, perhaps even leaving it on Jonty's bedside table as a surprise. As the girl worked her magic, Orlando subtly made enquiries about whether they produced regular commissions of this sort. His "uncle" might be interested in having such an exotic tribute every year on the anniversary of Auntie's funeral.

"I'm sure we could oblige." Miss Roberts was enthusiastic, although whether this was due to the thought of a nice regular income or because it pleased her customer wasn't clear. "Although it's not something we've done before, producing an annual tribute."

Disappointed at the loss of a lead, Orlando smiled, paid, took his flowers and left. He found a cab to take him to the duchess's house, but the lady he desired to see had gone to Bristol for the day—what was the great attraction of that city? He returned to the hotel and his notes, happily bearing the little surprise for his lover. And with the distinct wish that he could fly over the city in some great balloon, to make a note of all the glasshouses it harboured.

Jonty kept himself pretty well occupied up at the makeshift theatre. Jimmy proved polite and almost aloof, which gave him hope that the man might have at last got the message that he wasn't interested. Or, at least, if he was, that he wouldn't be giving in to temptation.

Jimmy asked him to work with the man playing the porter, to help the actor get all the comedy out of the words, then to advise Lady M. with some hints on how to play a lady of the nobility. "Imagine it's your mother you're trying to turn him into."

That remark certainly raised a smile on Jonty's face, as he believed some distinct connections could be made between Mrs. Stewart and the lady with the dagger. At least in terms of forceful behaviour, even if not in regard to a homicidal nature.

He became immersed in his work, managing to forget that Jimmy was in the offing, and enjoying himself greatly. As the afternoon began to slip into a balmy evening he at last received his leave. It was pleasant to take the chance of standing by a clump of trees next to the folly, looking out over the city to admire the mellow tones of the buildings as the sun's rays waxed orange and sent a gentle glow over them. He was lost in his thoughts of Orlando, of murder, of how to make Lady M. not sit in quite such a masculine manner, when he suddenly felt warm breath on the back of his neck.

"Lovely view, isn't it?"

Jonty could feel eyes boring into the back of his head and wondered to what the words referred. "Breathtaking," he replied, immediately regretting it. Too intimate a word by far.

"It'll be a lovely evening. Or could be." Jimmy laid his hand on his friend's shoulder, with just too much pressure to be the gesture of merely a friend.

Jonty stiffened. The implications of what had been said and done were unmistakable. Now all he had to do was show some degree of acquiescence and something would happen. A kiss, a caress; the very things he'd promised Orlando could never come to fruition. It would be so easy for the pair of them to turn, take a few paces and they would be out of sight of the company, then he'd just have to reach up, or Jimmy reach down, and their lips could touch.

He hadn't desired it back in London. They'd been good friends for a while, but no more than that. For Jonty the memories of the horrors at school and the untimely death of the man he loved were too close and vivid then—he'd not have been receptive to any romantic overtures. Overtures which, on sober reflection, must have been going on and to which he'd been entirely blind. He wasn't blind now. "I have to go."

"Go where?"

"I have things to do, Jimmy."

"That's the coward's way out. Either produce a valid reason why you have to go right now, or tell me that you're not interested. I know you can't lie to me, Jonty. You were always an open book for me to read, even when you were kidding other people." No hint of malice or threat sounded in Jimmy's voice, just an extraordinary affection. "If you can't do either, I'll know."

Jonty could neither move away nor turn to see his tormentor's face. "You'll know what?"

"Are you full of nothing except questions, Dr. Stewart? You must drive your students to distraction, like you're driving me. I'll know there's a chance, more than a chance, that you'll come back here and agree." Jimmy squeezed his friend's shoulder. "Agree to making it a lovely evening for the both of us."

Jonty couldn't be entirely sure, but he was fairly certain a pair of warm lips were at this point pressed briefly to the back of his neck, leaving a sensation that wouldn't pass away. He shrugged the hands off his back, mumbled an apology and left, not even glancing over his shoulder. At last he understood the imprecations in stories not to look back—not that the risk was being turned into a pillar of salt, but that what had been left behind might tempt you to turn around and be lost forever.

He walked swiftly, without thinking, until he was back in the hotel and engulfed in a delighted yet puzzled mathematician's arms.

"What's the matter?" Orlando held his lover close.

"Life." Jonty buried his nose in Orlando's jacket, nestling down like a kitten until he felt ready and able to talk. "I'm hardly spending any time with you, for a start. We'd anticipated we could at least be together for half the day but with this *Macbeth* thing it's all to pot. I should have realised. I've decided I'm not going to spend so much time helping with the play and I may not even appear in it, lure of the kilts notwithstanding."

Orlando could rarely disguise his feelings from his lover. Now his face suggested he knew he wasn't being told the entire truth. "Well, I think that's excellent news. Less time for old Smarmy Chops for one thing. What say we go down to the baths now, eh, Jonty? We can book a table for a late dinner—I'm sure those waters would do you the world of good."

Jonty smiled, some of the worry easing from his tense, weary shoulders. "That sounds wonderful, Orlando. A good warm soak, a walk back in the gloaming and a bottle of claret. I can't think of anything designed to better improve my mood." He rose, only to sit again, abruptly. "Actually, I can. Something just as warm as a bath and as succulent as claret." He took his lover's hand, traced the lines of the fingers. He shuddered at the remembrance of Jimmy's hands on his back, hoped—again— that Orlando wouldn't realise, couldn't guess at the shame which lay behind his sudden need to make love. The need to prove to himself that he only truly wanted Orlando.

"You're completely insatiable." Orlando's face suggested that wasn't a totally undesirable quality. "What would you have done if you'd felt the call of a monastery?"

"What a bizarre question. I don't think I've ever had any inclination for the cloistered life. Why on earth should you ask?"

"I was thinking of what it would have been like to be born in Shakespeare's day. I couldn't quite imagine you deposing Richard Burbage or Will Kemp, so I thought you might have been a monk."

"Orlando, you are an idiot. I won't even entertain that issue with an answer, other than this." Jonty pushed his lover towards the wall, encountering not the slightest resistance until Orlando was pressed tightly against the wallpaper. Jonty, several inches shorter than his lover but with muscles like a bull, could usually restrain him unless unfair tactics were involved. This time he used his strength to keep the man pinned while he assaulted his mouth with a series of fierce kisses, kisses which worked along the line of his neck until they were foiled by the stiff, starched collar.

"Take this off." Jonty jabbed at Orlando's shirt. "It's inhibiting the process."

Orlando was clearly trying not to grin. "As you wish, Brother Jonathan." He peeled off his jacket, then began to fiddle with his cufflinks.

"That monk joke is wearing rather thin." Jonty worked his way down the row of buttons, tugging at the fine silk vest which lay beneath. "I'm beginning to think of advantages, though, to the wearing of a simple habit. The issue of access for one thing—I mean, it's all very well when there's time and to spare, but for a man in a hurry this is all a bit of a palaver." He began to pull at Orlando's fly buttons. "See? Ridiculous."

"You are in a state, aren't you? I don't know what happened today but it's got you all fingers and thumbs." Orlando stopped short, perhaps aware that he'd somehow hit a raw nerve.

Jonty giggled, although for once guilt and nerves caused it, rather than the laughter which usually punctuated their lovemaking. "Those fingers and thumbs could be employed a lot more gainfully than fiddling with your buttons. They could be..." He insinuated his forefinger into the gap where he'd got one of the wretched things to open.

"Well, they could. Indeed." Orlando gasped for breath.

"And then they might..." Jonty wriggled the felonious little digits along his lover's waistband, found the small of his back and then sneaked them lower.

"Oh, yes. They might well." Orlando's voice was shaky, hoarse. "I think I should make the access easier for them." He undressed, moving gradually into his bedroom, pursued by an expert on the Bard who couldn't keep his lips or hands to himself. Then why should he, when Orlando's skin felt like silk, albeit downy silk, under his fingers?

"I do love you." Jonty drew his lover onto the bed, let himself be stripped, made himself prey to Orlando's roving hands. "No one but you makes me feel this way." *Perhaps I'm protesting too much. Perhaps I'm only trying to persuade myself that it's true.*

"Of course not. Coppersmith and Stewart—like Gonville and Caius." Orlando's hands worked down from his lover's waist, found their target, spent some time in languid delight. "I'm sorry to be the one doing the hurrying this time, but it had better be now, you know, or else it'll all be too late."

"I'm ready." Jonty was ready; body prepared ever since he'd

been railing at his lover's buttons. "Make it now, Orlando. Please."

Their union was all it normally was, a confirmation of their affection, an affirmation of their love despite all the world's condemnation, a sheer reckless delight. But the culmination, the concurrent climaxes of excitement, were tinged with the savour of guilt, something Jonty couldn't purge from his brain.

Chapter Seven

Jonty didn't notice the lilies until he went to find some clean underwear on Saturday morning.

"Are they the same sort? As the ones on the grave, I mean." Orlando stood in the doorway, his pyjamas looking ridiculously free of creases for garments which had just been slept in. There were times when Jonty wondered whether his lover habitually got up in the night and gave his clothes the once over with an iron.

"Similar, but not quite the same. A different variety, I should say." Jonty held the flowers to the light. "The ones in the graveyard alongside the roses had the merest hint of green to them, I think. And were a slightly different shape. I suspect that may corroborate your belief that they didn't come from the shop where your lady friends work." He carefully laid them down. "I can't remember you buying me flowers before."

"I did, that time when you had the flu. Only you were too ill to appreciate them." Orlando considered his feet, his usual displacement activity of shoe studying being unavailable due to the lack of the leathery substances. "Miss Peters understood that they meant something and said they could stay in the sick room. Not as fancy as these, just some late chrysanthemums..."

"I vaguely remember there being something rather striking in a vase when I came to. Although I'm afraid most of that time is rather muddled in my memory. Except," he added with his trademark grin all over his face, "that first kiss. Well, technically it wasn't our first kiss as that had taken place almost a year before, but it was very nice."

"It made you cough." Orlando's brow creased at the memory of what had been a very worrying time for them all.

"Well, I would imagine that you kissing a person could make anyone cough. You're a bit of all right, you know."

"Jonty! What sort of an expression is that to use? I guess it's one of Harding's little gems."

Jonty took up a cushion and smote his lover's head with it, partly so Orlando wouldn't notice he'd flushed with embarrassment. "Well it isn't, smarty pants. My dear papa once used it in reference to what he thought of Mama when he first saw her. I've been looking for the opportune moment to employ it ever since." He put down the cushion and poked his lover's chest with a particularly spiky finger—Orlando alleged that he sharpened them on the quiet. "And if you tell that to my mother, we'll all be for the high jump, you included, so I would resist all temptation to do so."

"I wouldn't presume. She's spanked me once, I don't want to increase the number of instances." Orlando stretched, going off to the bathroom with a muttered comment over his shoulder that *someone* didn't spank him nearly enough any more.

"I heard that. Wait until tonight. I'll soak my hands in vinegar to get them to the correct degree of hardness."

Jonty lay on the bed. There was no point in getting ready until Orlando had finished in the bathroom, and that could take an age if he felt so inclined. There had been a time, when they were first in love, that he'd taken very little time over his toilet. He'd always been spick and span, bright as a new pin, and his clothes must have been made of some substance over which dirt simply flowed then passed on, as he never had a speck on him. But in the matter of soaps or pomades or the various more modern versions of bay rum, he hadn't shown an interest.

That had all changed now; a bewildering variety of soaps and hair oils, among other things, graced Forsythia Cottage. There had been several occasions when Jonty would have been prepared to swear that Mrs. Ward had used the expression *smells like a tart's boudoir* under her breath in reference to their bathroom. Still, he reflected, it was all part of the Pygmalion process, Galatea growing up and becoming worldlier. It couldn't be denied that Orlando now smelled and looked wonderful, even more than he'd done when Jonty had first stolen the man's chair.

Nicer even than Jimmy Harding smelled, he thought, then quickly turned his attention to safer matters. Like the murder of Sarah Carter.

They'd decided to tackle Mr. Bredon in the afternoon, while the morning would involve Jonty in a little investigation following up his father's possible address for Thomas Critchley. The man supposedly lived in Bradford on Avon, which only required a brief train journey up the valley and a bit of luck about him being at home. And if at home, *at home.*

Jonty didn't need to make up an excuse for paying a call at such an unearthly hour. His father was convinced that the mere mention of Mrs. Stewart's name would prove a miraculous opener of unfriendly doors in this case. Eventually Jonty had to employ the same name—or the threat of reporting to it—to gain access to the bathroom and finish his own preparations for the day.

He and Orlando breakfasted on excellent bacon and sausages, then Jonty snuggled up with *The Telegraph* until it was a decent time to wander down to the station.

Bradford on Avon was a mere stone's throw to the east—Jonty had hardly sat down when it seemed he was getting up again and disembarking to go off in search of his quarry. Some careful enquiries of the porter, and a half-crown, produced a reasonable set of directions as to how to find the place, so Jonty swallowed hard and set off.

The house seemed impressive enough, as did the butler at the door, who informed him that Thomas Critchley was *at home*. Jonty's visiting card was taken, on the back of which he'd scribbled a few words mentioning his mother.

A moment later Critchley appeared, jovial and hearty, dispensing with the formality which demanded the butler should have taken a guest in, the host himself pumping Jonty's hand with enthusiasm. "You look just like your mother did in her twenties. My goodness she was a lovely little thing."

Jonty bit back a laugh at the word *little*.

"I'll hope you'll forgive me talking in such a familiar way. We were such great friends."

Jonty recalled some of the expressions his mother had used to describe this man; over-familiar had been one of the more polite ones. In her opinion he'd been outdone only by *that toe rag Parker* in the matter of attempting to take liberties. It didn't surprise Jonty at all that the man should have been associating with whores. He rather hoped that his mother had given Critchley the same hefty punch on the nose that she'd been prone to giving unwanted suitors. "She certainly remembers you." There was no doubt on that score.

"I do hope so. You must give her my fondest regards. And your father, too. Lucky man. Lucky man."

Coffee was offered and accepted, taken into a delightful conservatory awash with exotic plants, then the conversation turned for a while to the trivial, the doings of mutual acquaintances and the like.

"Mama would be impressed with these plants. She has many qualities, but green fingers aren't one of them." Jonty found Critchley quite pleasant to talk to—perhaps he had mellowed with age—and he began to make mental notes as they spoke. His mother was touching sixty, so this man must be the same. He would have been in his early thirties when the murder occurred, which was older than Gibbs the solicitor had been, if Orlando was any judge of age. Not, it turned out, some flighty youth sowing his wild oats, as most of the other men seemed to have been.

"If Mrs. Stewart hasn't green fingers, then I must confess that neither have I." Critchley swept his arm through an arc, encompassing the blooms. "I acquired a new manservant two years ago and this is the fruits of his labours."

Jonty knew he'd have to verify the timescale, but it seemed like a nice little theory—that Critchley grew the lilies—had been blown out of the water. The discussion moved more openly towards the nature of Jonty's business in Bath. Critchley was one of those who had read the article in *The Times* and soon asked whether the men had a case in hand. "It would be very useful to you, having this business with your manuscript, the play and your colleague's old books, to cover something up in the investigating line."

"It would, I must remember it. Yet the fact is that we came here with nothing but university business and a bit of sightseeing in mind. The matter of murder came afterwards." Jonty was gratified to see his host's eyebrows shoot up towards his receding hairline.

"Murder? A recent one?"

"No. This case is an old one, although the commission is

new. Dr. Buckner's son wishes us to examine a killing which took place at the House of Sulis." Jonty carefully noted all of Critchley's reactions. "This took place twenty-five years ago and I have to admit that's one of the reasons I'm here now. To ask you what you know about it."

"Sarah Carter." His host spoke quietly and without emotion. He'd shown no real surprise since murder had first been mentioned.

"Yes. You obviously remember the young lady."

"I do. She was a very special girl." Critchley rose. "Please allow me to ring for some more coffee and then I'll tell you all I know." He twitched the bell pull and, when the butler had come and gone, he spoke. "We were a group of five. I suppose you already know that but I shall verify it for you. Myself, Jeremy Weir—he's been dead a while now—Phillip Gibbs, who's a solicitor in the city, Derek Bredon—he's still living here too but I'm not sure what he does with himself—and Derek's friend Brian Appleby. Does that accord with what you'd been told?"

"It does and I am grateful for that last name. No one else seemed to know it. Or at least admit to knowing it."

"That'll be Gibbs being deliberately obtuse, I'll warrant, or else losing his marbles. We were all pals together in those days. Jeremy was fond of that Carter girl, but I was particularly friendly, as you might say, with another one of them. Her real name I can't tell you as she never disclosed it, although we all called her Adelaide." A wistful look crossed Critchley's face. "She had a real touch of class about her."

"Do you know where either Appleby or Adelaide are now?" Jonty took out his trusty notepad and pen to ensure he kept a record of everything for Orlando's inevitable cross examination. At least he had the name of the third girl now, although he wasn't sure what good it would do them; it wasn't as if they had any idea where to look for her.

"Brian and I lost touch with one another some twenty years ago. I will freely admit that we failed to see eye to eye over something and we never reached a rapprochement. The girl's whereabouts? I wouldn't have the slightest idea, although Bredon might, if you can catch up with him." Critchley had a sly look in his eye but he refused to elucidate on the strange remark.

Jonty felt confused about just which man was *attached* to which doxy; he wondered if it varied according to the occasion. "Were you friendly with the other two 'ladies'?"

"Not especially. I mean I talked to them but I never...employed their services. We all held parties together, both at the House of Sulis and elsewhere, so it was inevitable that we would converse. Sometimes we were really quite respectable in our behaviour."

Jonty wished that his mother was present to give the man a piece of her mind. "So who was Sarah's particular friend then?"

"That would be the late Jeremy Weir, second son of a very distinguished family and unlikely to have inherited the title of duke, his brother being so hale and hearty. His mother still lives here in Bath, now that his father has gone the way of all flesh. Bredon was fond of the girl too, although he usually got left with Clarissa, if he could peel her away from Gibbs." He stopped talking, considered Jonty carefully. "You don't approve of this, do you? This talk of loose morals. That's your father coming out."

Jonty decided he didn't need his mama's presence. He would finish the interview and then punch this man's unctuous leer back down his throat, all on his own. "How did you know this was the murder I was referring to? Everyone else had assumed or been told the story about natural causes."

"You can't catch me like that. Brian had his suspicions right from the start. He'd have been happy to make a fuss but we all persuaded him otherwise. I rather suspect that was at the root of our crucial argument—he always plumped for the truth rather than what was expedient."

"Did you know that Sarah Carter was married, or who her husband was?"

"I'd heard something along those lines although I'm not sure I believed it." Critchley suddenly stopped, fixing his interrogator with a strange look. "You know about the child, of course?"

Jonty couldn't stop himself from showing surprise at this unexpected development. "Child? Her husband's I assume?"

"Who knows? I have only the sketchiest knowledge of the matter, but I would wish you to know about it in case it proves relevant to your investigation. When I say child, I'm afraid that I mislead you—it was never born. Brian told me, not long after her death, that Sarah Carter had lost a child early in her pregnancy, if you'll excuse what is regarded as an indelicate term. The story was that she'd had a miscarriage, but he implied that she may have deliberately got rid of the child, perhaps under duress from the father or his family."

"Dear God…" Jonty was genuinely shocked. He knew that such things went on—his mother's charitable institution for unfortunate girls housed more than one who had been forced down that route—yet he was appalled. When he thought of how much his sister Lavinia yearned for a baby and how unlikely it was that she would ever conceive one, given her aversion to matters carnal, it cut him to the quick that some poor unwanted babe had been disposed of.

Critchley noticed the distress caused to his guest and

softened his approach somewhat. He'd no doubt meant to shock, to show off his inside knowledge regarding the girl, but he'd genuinely upset his visitor. "I know. It turns anyone's heart to hear of such things, but they have gone on since time immemorial and I dare say they always will. Men and women will lie together and they must accept the consequences."

Jonty didn't want to be mollified. He bit his lip so that he wouldn't make the rejoinder about *one party naturally suffering more than the other* which was springing so readily to his mind. "When was this?"

"Appleby told me just before we had our estrangement..."

"No, I mean when had Sarah Carter lost her child?"

"It would have been in the early eighties. Perhaps the year she died or the one before, I am not entirely sure. Ask Brian, he might have a better memory of events than I do."

"But I don't know where to find him."

"Bredon will know. Bredon seems to know everything."

Jonty finished making his notes, thanked his host, then set off back towards the station, ruminating. Near the bridge someone had put a poster on a notice board announcing the production of *Macbeth,* and Jonty's thoughts, which had been kept firmly away from the matter of Jimmy Harding, suddenly began to wander again. He couldn't get on the train back to Bath without making his mind absolutely clear.

For all that he kept telling himself he wasn't interested, Jimmy's smiling face kept appearing in his noddle, slyly suggesting that he really was tempted. *If you'd only be honest with yourself then you'll find you'd really like to snuggle up to me for a little while.*

It was like being in the middle of a court case. No sooner had Jimmy spoken than Orlando would stand up and begin the case for the defence. *You've only ever loved me—well, over the past two years only me—we're joined for life and no one should be allowed to come between us.*

He imagined Inspector Wilson being called as a corroborative witness. *Young Dr. Stewart should set his mind to detection, not dalliance.*

He kept walking, not really registering where his feet took him, back and forth through the centre of the little town. *Every case we've tackled has brought us under threat. There hasn't been a nice juicy murder which has accompanied a period of calm in our lives.* Prosecution counsel Coppersmith was addressing the bench and he was right, as usual.

The first case, the St. Bride's Murders as the baser corners of the press still referred to it—or the college next door's Junior Common Room, which was even viler—had culminated in a threat to Jonty's life. The killing of Charles Ainslie had coincided with them taking their love out into the world at large, learning how to hide their enormous affection for each other behind a façade of friendship.

Ah, m'lud, my learned friend is mistaken. Counsel for the defence spoke up in his pleasing American tones. *That can't be applied to the Woodville Ward case.*

True, there had been no personal danger then, although it had come to them as a result of Orlando's accident. *My lord, that was even worse for the accused—weeks of uncertainty about whether we would ever regain our love and intimacy of the previous year. Worst of all, our latest case threatened Dr. Stewart's sanity itself. Yet we overcame even that together and emerged happier, healthier.*

Of course we did, or else I wouldn't feel so guilty just for thinking about Jimmy.

And now? Dr. Stewart isn't in any physical or mental danger, m'lud.

Jonty didn't need the prosecution counsel to answer that. The risk was one of them breaking every vow they'd made to each other. To be more specific, that *he* would break every vow. Orlando would never contemplate adultery even for a moment.

The appearance of the word *adultery* in his brain made Jonty pull up short, seeing clearly who'd be on the bench—Lord Justice Mr. Stewart, and what would he say if he knew his youngest son was even contemplating a dalliance? For all that he and Orlando hadn't spoken vows in St George's chapel, where all the other Stewarts had held their nuptials, Jonty was, in his father's eyes, as firmly allied to Orlando as Lavinia was to her Ralph. And Mr. Stewart would say that the same applied to God's point of view. Adultery it would surely be.

Jonty sighed, shaking himself as if he could shake off the demons haunting his thoughts. He had to get his head down on his book, get on with the case and ignore every overture Jimmy made. It was as simple and as difficult as that.

As he dragged himself down to the station, the theme of rivalry flooded his bewildered brain. Orlando's rival, the Rival Poet, rivals for the throne of Scotland, rivals for the favours of common prostitutes. Wherever he turned he found enmity and competition. He suddenly felt quite sure that the key to Sarah Carter's death would lie in some sort of contention, the opposition of dominant wills. He had no concrete evidence for such a theory, yet it felt right.

He was also aware that his will-it-ever-be-finished treatise on the sonnets was sorely lacking a pithy page or two about the identity of the rival poet. His butterfly thoughts took off in the direction of *great reckonings in little rooms* and wondered whether a certain suite at the Grand Hotel would soon be witnessing the verbal equivalent of one of those, concerning Orlando and his adversary.

His thoughts flitted back to his precious sonnets, to the turmoil the Bard had felt over the straying affections of his dark lady. Orlando would be thinking the same every time his lover looked at the attractive American. A wave of guilt swept over him, making his pace quicken. He had to get back to Bath, he had to find Orlando and kiss him, or whatever would be allowed in the place where they encountered each other. He needed to reassure the man that he really was the only one who mattered.

Perhaps in doing so Jonty could reassure *himself* that particular fact was true.

Chapter Eight

"Jonty, what are you doing?" Orlando at last managed to break his lover's embrace and take a breath.

"Kissing you, you big oaf. Because I love you and I suspect I don't tell you enough."

If Orlando had been more of a student of the Bard he might have recognised this as a distinct case of *the gentleman doth protest too much*, but he wasn't and he didn't. He was simply grateful that he'd come back to his room to change his shirt, having found a greasy mark on it, so had been met by his lover there rather than in a public place. The hug had been hot and passionate, such as was rarely now produced during the hours of daylight. It was very pleasant, if a bit disconcerting.

"How was your morning? Successful?" Orlando held Jonty at arm's length so he could analyse, from his face, the likely answer. He was pleased to see enough enthusiasm to suggest he had stuff to share.

"I think so. There's certainly a clearer picture emerging of the dynamics within the two groups. And there's a very juicy little piece of information in re Miss or Mrs. Carter." Jonty raised his hand to stifle all further questioning. "But I refuse to divulge it until I'm outside a decent bit of lunch. Then I'll tell all."

Which he did, slurping down mock turtle soup and

following it with a nice piece of Dover sole. Orlando rather dramatically dropped his spoon at the mention of the child and felt convinced, as Jonty swore he did as well, that this would prove to be a crucial factor. At last they had something which gave the inkling of a motive, something their conversation had naturally turned to, on and off, since they'd first received their commission.

"Why would anyone deliberately murder a prostitute—" Orlando spoke the last word almost beneath his breath, "—in circumstances where the crime might not remain hidden or unsolved? This doesn't seem to be some Jack the Ripper type."

Jonty attacked his fruit salad as if it might be tortured into yielding all the secrets to the case. He too kept his voice low in case he shocked any old ladies, who might then report him to his mother. "There certainly seems to be only this *one* murder." They knew that for a fact because Buckner had kept an eye out in case there had been similar cases reported, either here in Bath or in nearby Bristol.

"You've kept saying the motivation had to be a personal one. Clever clogs."

They'd already considered the rationales they'd come across in the past—vengeance on a type, retribution for a particular affront, calculated murder to cover one's tracks, many and varied motives. None of those seemed to apply this time, unless there was some connection between the dead girl and her clients that was more than commercial.

"If it's a matter of hatred or revenge, then it seems likely that her killer was one of the other prostitutes." Not that Orlando had much—or indeed any—understanding of this class of girl.

Yet a child, a child who had died *in utero* or been done away with, that would bring in all sorts of possibilities. Jonty began to mark them off on his fingers. "The baby obviously had a father, and if we assume it wasn't Mr. Carter, then it might have been one of those present that night. It's a long shot, but I can just imagine a father who'd been horrified to find out about the loss of his offspring becoming so mad that he might strike out at the person who'd destroyed his child."

"And do you know—" Orlando waved his spoon, like he waved a pen at his students when trying to get them to understand integral calculus, "—if the baby isn't linked to the murder, then it might explain why someone still sends flowers to the girl's grave."

"You're a genius. A mutual loss, if the child really did miscarry, might have made a particular bond between Sarah and one of her gentlemen."

"That mysterious husband of hers may well still have a role here." The new information had opened all sorts of avenues of possibilities in Orlando's eager brain. "If he came home and found her expecting, he might have made her get rid of it and then he could have taken a long-planned revenge."

"Do you think the killer was very clever or just very lucky? Do you suppose he or she might well have been confident that they wouldn't be caught, for whatever reason?"

"If he was one of those with influence among the authorities he might well have felt it worth chancing his arm. Which seems to eliminate Mr. Carter, if that really was his name and if his social status is as we've assumed."

"Orlando." Jonty laid down his glass of water. "Does it have to be one of the people present at the baths? The murderer, I mean? Couldn't it be someone who came in while all hell was breaking loose? As both Gibbs and Dr. Buckner himself said, it was fairly frantic when he returned—people flitting about and trying to make their exits before they were recognised, the doctor arguing with the colleague who'd let the place run to the dogs, screaming and protesting girls everywhere. I wonder if anyone could have come in? Or if they'd already been hiding in the building and used the chaos to cover their escape?"

"We should ask Buckner junior." Orlando's eyebrows twitched, a sure sign that he was thinking. "And we haven't really looked at the layout of the place, tried to work out how easy it would have been to move about within the complex. As you said, it's a bit of a labyrinth."

"Let's go now then." Jonty rose and reached for his wallet. "My shout today. I'll take a cab up to the rehearsals when we're done. I suppose I have to go, even though I'd rather be sleuthing, and then you can go and pin down your mysterious Mr. Bredon. I'm sure he has some important stuff to convey."

📖

The baths were busy, it being Saturday afternoon and most people's business finished with for the day. Millar had been rather alarmed that he wouldn't be able to accommodate their needs, but when he'd had it discreetly explained what they were about, he was more than happy to see that they had all they required, which was in effect the free run of the place for a while. He knew of the Sarah Carter case and had been told to offer the gentlemen any assistance they might require in solving it. Buckner junior himself wasn't present; he too had gone off to Bristol, that Mecca of the West Country towards which all men seemed to gravitate.

Millar couldn't show them the exact place the body had been found. That area had been reconfigured a year after the event, because it held such sad associations for Buckner senior and was possibly having an inhibiting effect on the House of

Sulis regaining its position as a bathing establishment of quality.

As Jonty had pointed out on their first visit, the atrium led down to the changing rooms, which was the hub of the institution. From there doors led off to the main pool, the steam room, the tepidarium and the frigidarium. Each of these had at least one smaller room or cupboard abutting onto them, to contain cleaning or other equipment, which couldn't be left to pollute the view for refined customers.

The cupboard where Sarah Carter had been found naked and strangled had been opened up to provide a niche in which a statue of Niobe provided a tasteful remembrance to the girl. Back then, to have reached it from the main door would have involved crossing the atrium, the changing rooms and the frigidarium itself. Why the victim should have gone there of her own or anyone else's volition was beyond them.

"Is there another entrance to the House of Sulis? Even a window which might have been used to gain access?" Jonty had got it into his mind that the killer had come from outside; his intuition had proved accurate before, so he felt it worth exploring every avenue.

"There is a small back door, used for deliveries and the like, but no gentleman would think to use it."

Orlando turned and studied the wall, so that Millar couldn't see his smile; the man would have been horrified to know what gentlemen would think to do.

"Could someone have made their way in through it? Someone determined not to be noticed?" Jonty was as persistent as a dog with a bone at times.

"If you'll beg my pardon, sir, I'd say that route would be much more likely to attract attention. Let me explain. There's always been a desk in the atrium and behind that a door into another room. I use it as a rest area or to make coffee and snacks or to let the cleaning ladies put their feet up. A hundred and one things. That's where the back door gives onto—there's usually someone in there and if not, someone's sitting at the desk. Dr. Buckner always insists that there are two of us in the offing in case of an accident. One to fetch help and the other to mind the fort."

"But this is now, Mr. Millar. We're talking about twenty-five years ago." Orlando frowned at what he perceived to be the man's obtuseness.

"It would have been worse then, sir. There might have been half a dozen servants coming and going from that room, fetching things for the gentlemen and their 'guests', especially in the time *the other man* had the run of the place. I'd say that if you had enough luck and timed it right, you could come through the front door, bold as brass, get into the changing rooms, then...well, with all those little booths, you could hide until it was quiet."

Orlando wondered whether it would be worth locating some of those servants. They'd have been even better placed to wander in and out of the changing rooms. "Did the ladies—I use the term guardedly—change in the same place as the gentlemen?" Orlando couldn't keep the disapproval from his voice.

"I believe so. I wasn't here in those days, thank the Lord. Not the sort of goings-on I'd have liked to be associated with."

"And were all those rooms entirely empty when all the knaves had been turfed out that infamous night?" Jonty's eyes shone bright, as if he had just worked out the meaning of some obscure phrase in *Hamlet*.

"As I understand it, sir. Dr. Buckner had made a point of making sure they took all their belongings with them. Why do you ask?"

"Because Sarah Carter was found unclothed. Someone must have taken her dress and shoes away, quite deliberately." Jonty looked at his friend. "Lilies on a grave, clothes that disappear into the night, a child that did the same. They're the keys, Orlando, be sure of it."

📖

"I wasn't certain you were going to show up." Jimmy was grinning broadly but his eyes showed that he must have been genuinely anxious.

"I did say it would be nearer three o'clock than two." Jonty smiled in return but he was trying not to appear too enthusiastic.

"Oh, I didn't mean that. I was feeling a bit guilty about yesterday." Jimmy looked ashamed of himself. "I wanted to talk to you, alone, before we get down to the business of the day and I'm not going to repeat my mistake of being so forward. I've been in agony—convinced myself that you'd never darken the sham doorstep of the Sham Castle again. I rather put the pressure on you, didn't I?"

"You did rather. I felt like I was being grilled by Mama about the matter of a cake missing from the pantry." Jonty began to relax; all the way up to the rehearsals he'd been screwing up his courage and was relieved to find that Jimmy seemed to have cooled his ardour somewhat. It would make the whole thing at least workable and bearable.

"I have to ask. I hope you won't think me too bold, but you seem very devoted to Dr. Coppersmith. Would that be a fair summation of things?"

Jonty sighed. "It would. He's all the world to me, Jimmy."

"Then he's a very lucky man to be held in such esteem. I wish that I'd found someone to be my lifelong companion—which might be a bit of a presumption on my part regarding your relationship?" Jimmy looked young and vulnerable, as he had so many years previously, back at University College.

Jonty patted his friend's arm in what he hoped was a brotherly fashion. "I've been very fortunate in finding him, I know."

"Then I'll say no more than to promise that if you ever get tired of him and want to hitch your horse to another wagon—well, don't look so shocked, I'm an American!—then I'd be proud to take over the reins." Jimmy laughed and Jonty followed his example, for the first time feeling at ease in the man's company.

"Now to business, sir, and it's little short of an emergency. I have a leading man who is at the dentist with a cracked tooth at present so I'm having to rehearse act two, scene two with me as the man himself, and it's a challenge." He lowered his voice. "Especially as the leading lady is playing up a bit. He may look the part—as a woman he's nothing short of sensational—but he's not quite getting the dialogue. Could I prevail upon you, I know it's a huge burden, to say the lady's words as they were intended to be spoken and not like you're a washerwoman touting for business?" Jimmy beamed, his glorious smile ensuring that Jonty couldn't find it in his heart to refuse.

Jonty only hoped, as he wrapped a shawl about his waist to give at least the tiniest allusion of being female, that his father shouldn't happen to walk past. Or Nurse Hatfield. Or worst of all, Orlando.

He had his book, although he knew the part fairly well, and also had it clear in his mind how the lines should be played, having seen an excellent Lady M. or two in his youth. Nicholas Caddon, the man who'd been appointed to play the part, sat at the edge of the stage still scowling, not having been mollified by his director, who'd spoken of a *world renowned expert, lucky to have his input, just while Simon's getting his tooth done.*

Jimmy had been entirely correct in his description. The man really did look like a Shakespearian heroine. The assumption of a dress and a bit of makeup would complete the illusion very well, although still leaving everyone aware it was a man in the role.

"That which hath made them drunk hath made me bold." Jonty entered from stage left, looking suitably determined. "What hath quench'd them hath given me fire..." He carried on, taking the speech at a good pace and setting up the leading man's entrance.

"Who's there! What, ho!" Jimmy spoke the words well, not sounding to Jonty's ear—as one particularly annoying amateur Macbeth had—like he was inviting people to a game of tennis. Jimmy was stationed behind the castle, awaiting his cue to enter. When it came he was suitably dramatic and Jonty hastened across to grasp his arm.

"My husband!" That phrase rather stuck in Jonty's craw, but he was courageous and kept his gaze steady.

"I have done the deed..."

The actors pressed on. Everyone, including the reluctant Nicholas, who appeared to be starting grudgingly to approve, was transfixed by the intensity with which the scene was being played.

"I could not say 'Amen'." Jimmy was ensconced in the part, sweat breaking from his brow. "When they did say 'God bless us!'"

"Consider it not so deeply." Jonty gently touched the other man's face, then hastily withdrew his hand. He hoped the watching players would simply think this the most subtle of gestures. More interchanges followed, leading on inexorably to the part where Jonty grabbed at the little props in Jimmy's hands, spat out, "Infirm of purpose! Give me the daggers", then spoke the rest of the speech while slowly withdrawing behind the castle again, the last few words, "For it must seem their guilt", fading as he disappeared behind the stonework.

Rapturous applause broke out, cries of "Bravo!" and a rather confused one of "Brava!" greeting a red-faced Jonty as he poked his nose back around the scenery. "Was that all right?"

"It was marvellous. Just the sort of passion we should be investing all the play with. What do you think, Nicholas?" Jimmy was positively beaming.

"Amazing." Caddon's face shone with enthusiasm; he'd been well and truly won over. "I think I see things much more clearly now. May I try the scene?"

"Of course. Dr. Stewart, could I have those daggers back? And the shawl for Nicholas to wrap himself in?" Jimmy smiled winningly and let his friend escape to watch the reworking of the scene in Caddon's hands.

The man had certainly grasped what this was all about—Jonty could hear murmurs of appreciation around him and the muttered words *transformation, much better, miraculous change.* He joined in the hearty applause at the end; even Orlando was going to find it hard to criticise this production.

The sudden appearance of huge kettles and a veritable fleet of cups and saucers, from the miniature field kitchen Jimmy had hired to deal with the company's catering needs, brought the rehearsal to a halt and allowed people to compare notes.

"How did you do it, Jonty? Get so quickly into her character?" Jimmy was stirring huge quantities of sugar into his tea, eyes bright with excitement.

Jonty wondered if his pleasure was due to the excellent

acting that had been on display, his own foray into the leading man's role or something else he didn't want to name. "I simply thought of both Mama and my grandmother. Neither of them would have hesitated should the circumstances have required them to replicate Lady M.'s deeds."

"Truly? They must be formidable ladies indeed." Caddon bubbled with something Jonty hoped was simply admiration for his family.

"They are. Or I should say *was* in the case of my much lamented grandmother. They'd have sorted out anyone who needed to be dealt with—if the pair of them had been at Hastings, England would never have turned Norman."

"They sound rather frightening. How could such a dam have produced such an offspring?" Jimmy shook his head in mock wonder.

"Oh, the gauntlet of iron hides a fist of silk. They'd not have used brute force, either of them. Charm and persuasion and an absolute sense of being right. It's a potent combination to confront anyone with."

"But one of the points about Lady M. is surely..." Caddon lowered his voice as there were tea ladies in the vicinity, "...her sex appeal. She exerts a special power over her husband that must be associated with their carnal relations."

Jimmy raised an eyebrow, caught Jonty's eye. Both men were shocked, not by what was said—it was what any sensible scholar might say of the Bard's work—but in its implications towards the Stewart females. And towards the two people who'd just been acting the scene.

Caddon immediately grasped his *faux pas* and seemed to regret it. "Oh I say, I didn't mean to imply that your mother... I mean, steady on..." The man's face turned a more magnificent shade of crimson than even Orlando could manage.

Jonty laughed. "No offence intended so none taken, Mr. Caddon. And you're quite right in your judgment on Lady M. She uses her feminine wiles to every purpose. That's why an asexual woman in the part, all aggression or nobility or ambition, leaves me feeling something is lacking. She has to attract her husband and use that fact to manipulate him. Wouldn't you agree, Jimmy? Jimmy?"

"Sorry." The director seemed taken aback. "I was miles away, thinking about costumes."

Jonty wasn't sure that was the truth. By accident they'd strayed onto dangerous ground again, just as they'd done when lost in character on the stage. There'd been a sexual tension present then, even if it had manifested itself in nothing more than an excellent performance. He wondered exactly where Jimmy's thoughts had strayed.

Jonty suddenly felt the need to be doing something, anything, that could keep his brain distracted. "I think I should find that porter and go through his part a further time."

"Indeed." Jimmy looked about for the player in question, a local sprig of nobility whose father had talked the director into taking him on, giving the lad something productive to do for a few weeks. "And could you look at some of these costumes. They've at last arrived and I'm concerned about their authenticity. Looks more like Drury Lane than Glamis."

"My pleasure. If we don't catch each other later, I'll see you again on Monday afternoon?"

Jimmy nodded. "We need to get things moving in earnest then. Only a week to the dress rehearsal and then the first night a week on Monday." He sighed. "Well, at least they all know the words even if they don't know how to say them."

Orlando turned the corner with no great hopes. Twice more he'd tried to catch the elusive Mr. Bredon, calling in on the off chance only to be frustrated, and he wasn't optimistic about the supposedly lucky third time. He knocked on the door of Bredon's house and was amazed to find he'd at last returned from Bristol and was more than pleased to talk about the affair at the House of Sulis.

Orlando took his usual straight-at-'em approach; if they were to get anywhere with this case they needed to establish some more hard facts. Over the inevitable tea, this time served with a rather nice Dundee cake, Bredon opened his heart, or at least appeared to do so. He remembered the death of the girl, hadn't been suspicious at the time but equally wasn't surprised now that murder was being suggested. He'd been fond of Sarah Carter.

Funny, Orlando reflected, how everyone had said they were fond of this girl and yet there'd been someone who hated her enough to kill her.

"We used to keep company with another young woman, too. Clarissa. She was a real peach. I kept in touch with her for years. You must understand, Dr. Coppersmith, that for me I sought and enjoyed the companionship, and pleasant talk, as much as the physical side of things. I rarely indulged in that direction, just liked the company of girls who weren't necessarily being egged on by their mothers into assessing one's potential as a husband. In my youth it was like being in the silver ring, if you'll forgive the analogy. All I wanted was a woman who wasn't on the make."

Orlando wondered what these girls were if not *on the make*. "There was a third girl, Adelaide. Do you know what happened to her?"

"Clarissa told me that she'd been whisked off to the continent by some well-to-do patron. She always was a classy girl and I suppose she might have ended up presiding over a nice little *pension* somewhere." There was a shrewd look in his eye. "Does your question really mean 'Do I think she killed Sarah Carter'?"

"You can take it to mean that, if you think the answer will move the case forward."

"Only you can decide that, Dr. Coppersmith, I can only say what I know. The Adelaide I remember wouldn't have hurt a fly."

"A fly maybe. What about Sarah Carter?"

There was a pause before Bredon answered. "I don't think Adelaide would have had any reason to kill her, either."

Orlando changed tack, but found Bredon had little new to offer on the relationships or character of the other men, apart from the mysterious Appleby. He'd corresponded with him regularly—although they rarely met—until only a few years previously. Appleby had, some two or three years after the cleansing of the House of Sulis, entered a seminary and was now a priest, at which revelation Orlando nearly dropped his Dundee cake. "And you can think of no connection other than *the obvious* between Sarah and any of these men?" It wasn't quite the question he wanted to ask, but it covered his confusion. Somehow, the last thing he expected of any of these fellows was that they would take holy orders.

"Jeremy Weir was very fond of her. I suspect that if she'd been of a higher social status then he'd have been keen to marry her."

Orlando had already such a tight grip on his plate of cake that this latest revelation didn't destabilise it. "Did he know she was supposed to be already married?"

Bredon shrugged. "That I don't know—if he did, he didn't tell me at the time. I only heard that story years afterwards, from Clarissa. In retrospect it might have explained some of the things Jeremy said, or at least reinterpreted them."

"Can you elucidate this, please?" Orlando was trying to make notes, to be amalgamated with the ones he and Jonty already had. He liked things to be orderly; his lover was the sort of slut who could cope with higgledy piggledy, but he couldn't.

"Let me take you back twenty-five years, Dr. Coppersmith. You say the matter of murder was all covered up and that includes keeping things secret from some of those present. Jeremy and I had no idea that Sarah had died until the day before her funeral. We'd stayed well clear of the House of Sulis and the other places we met the girls. Brian Appleby told us she'd died, and Clarissa had told him. She'd formally identified the body at the inquest, or what must have passed for an inquest given what you've told me of Dr. Buckner's suspicions."

"Did you send flowers to her funeral?"

"The three of us, yes. At my instigation. We didn't attend— we dared not at the time. Call it cowardice, a wish not to lose our good name, whatever you want, but we sent our respects as best we could."

"And do you still send flowers?"

Bredon looked puzzled. "No. We only did it that one time, as far as I know. Does someone, then?"

"Every year as we understand it. Roses or hothouse lilies."

"Extraordinary. Well I guess it could be Appleby, though I'm not sure why he should. Jeremy died not long after Sarah, so it can't be him. I'm sorry, I'm not being much use, am I?"

"It would be very helpful if you could tell me what Mr. Weir said that you think could be...reinterpreted, I think that was the word?"

Bredon nodded. "It must have been a few days after the funeral, he was very low and in his cups. He was saying how he wished he could have married Sarah, how he would have done, had circumstances been different. I assumed at the time he meant if she'd been a baronet's daughter rather than a whore. Perhaps he wasn't really concerned about that at all, it was her being already married which provided the barrier."

"Did he say anything that might have implied he knew about her child?"

Bredon shook his head. "He said nothing at the time and I wouldn't have pressed him as I, again, only discovered many years later that Sarah had been pregnant."

"Sarah Carter was said to have lost that baby at some point in the year or so before her death, possibly intentionally. Could it have been the offspring of one of you three?"

"It could have been—biologically, if you understand me. You're never implying that any of us would have coerced her into disposing of it? We may not have been pure in body or soul but all three of us held life as sacred—such a thing would have been abhorrent." Bredon stopped, looking directly at Orlando. "I might be inclined to be searching for that husband of Sarah's if I were you."

"Perhaps." Orlando appreciated the logic in the point, except that they had nowhere to start. If they eliminated all other options then at least they could present Buckner junior with a half-answered case and would have to come back later in search of the elusive sailor, or whoever he was. If they went off on wild-goose chases now, they might have nothing to show for a fortnight's work. He rose to go. "Thank you for your help. May I return if necessary? And may I have an address for Father Appleby?"

He received acquiescence for the first although not for the

second. Bredon could only produce an address for several years previously; in the interim the man had been out in Africa and hadn't been in touch when, or indeed if, he'd returned.

As he shook his visitor's hand, Bredon considered Orlando's face intensely. "There are things which I could tell you but I wouldn't seek to influence your investigation. When you've spoken to everyone you can find who was present that night, then come back and see me."

Orlando nodded then set off down the steps to the street. Only when he'd trudged back to his hotel did he realise he should have asked where the floral tribute for the funeral had come from.

Chapter Nine

Saturday evening Jonty retired to their suite to sit with his manuscript, feeling a bit guilty. The sentiment was fast becoming an old friend. This time he felt bad because he'd spent more time thinking about Jimmy Harding than his book on the sonnets. He'd incorporated the magnificent first sentence he'd come up with when first wandering about Bath, but he'd done very little of consequence since.

Dinner, taken earlier with Orlando, had proved very pleasant, as all the meals they'd taken at the Grand had been. As the pair of them had taken coffee, a gentleman approached to ask if one or other of them might like to make up a hand of bridge as their usual fourth had gone to bed with a chill. Orlando was no great fan of bridge, preferring his whist, but had been without a decent card game for what seemed so long—at least a fortnight—that, after checking with Jonty, he'd agreed happily.

Jonty smiled in reminiscence of how alarmed the elderly gentleman had looked when he'd said he needed to get his head down over some sonnets. He'd had to explain, for what seemed like hours, that he didn't write them, only analysed them. "A poor profession but mine own." Only he wasn't doing a very good job at it, what with the combined distractions of a murder, *Macbeth* and Jimmy bloody Harding.

Now, if Orlando wanted to play bridge, that really was a nudge to his conscience that he should use the time to thrash about with the problems of jealousy between the threesome of the Bard, the dark lady and person unknown.

He opened his beloved book of sonnets and began to make notes, gradually becoming more and more pleased with himself. If there was one positive aspect to the heart wringing which was affecting him, it was getting some appreciation of what was going on within that triangle of love and jealousy, something he'd never had any understanding of before.

He worked on, his eyes beginning to sting and his body being vaguely aware that he was reaching that state his mother would describe as dangerously overtired. He wrote some final notes to pick up the next day—he felt confident now that the concluding part of the puzzle was close to being put in place— then put on his pyjamas, not actually sure that he would be able to get to sleep, despite the soporific effects of the works of Charles Dickens.

📖

Sunday morning Jonty lay in his bath, sweat breaking out on his forehead not just at the heat of the water but at the recollections of what had happened. He'd been unable to sleep, lying in the strange half state that was neither sleep nor waking, had become bothered by Orlando snoring at his side, had felt restless and confused, then decided to take some fresh air. He'd slipped on his clothes without really realising what was going on, stepped out into the cool evening and straight into the path of Jimmy, who might just have been lurking around the hotel entrance, the promptness with which he appeared.

It was so lovely, right from the moment Jimmy took his

hand so boldly right out on Great Pulteney Street, their fingers gently entwining and forming a Gordian knot which couldn't be broken by any amount of forbidding looks from those who were still treading the pavements. They wandered along in a daze, reaching Jimmy's own hotel and pressing onwards through the hall, climbing the stairs, entering the bedroom, all oblivious to whether anyone might be looking at them or speculating about their motives. They were hardly discreet—arm in arm they might have managed to maintain the illusion of mere friendship, but hand in hand should mean only one thing to those who saw it.

They were barely through the door before Jimmy pressed his friend up against the wall, hot breath sweet in his face, smiling like a child who's received all he could possibly want for his birthday. "I've waited so long, so very long. All these years I've thought of you, hoping that you might feel the same."

Jonty couldn't reply, couldn't force a sound from his throat, merely leaned in and surrendered to the kiss. And such a kiss. The first ones he'd shared with Orlando had been just gentle brushings of the lips, like the touch of a butterfly, all gallantry and tentativeness. This was completely different, mouth open from the start, tasting, probing, consuming.

Jimmy's lips tasted hot and sweet. He pressed himself slowly against Jonty's unresisting frame, hands roaming over his body, pulling his shirt free from his waistband, finding flesh and caressing it.

He was more passionate than either of Jonty's other loves had been during their first time; mad and wild were hardly adequate words for what went on.

It had all ended too soon, when Jonty had woken up and felt not Jimmy but Orlando at his side.

His initial feeling at realising it had all been a dream—

brought on by too many sonnets and not enough of the sobering effects of Dickens—had been a mixture of extreme relief and bitter disappointment, followed by a wave of disgust that could only be overcome by running a scalding hot bath and immersing himself in it, trying to rinse away all the sensations that had so thrilled and revolted him.

Lead us not into temptation. Maybe he'd never really understood the paternoster before now; all the promises he'd made to Orlando had been easy to fulfil so far. Jonty had always had the sneaking feeling that nuns and monks, and any other enclosed orders there might be, had life pretty easy in some ways. Loving your neighbour was a doddle if you never had to have contact with them. So with temptation—very simple to resist if you never came across it.

Now it was staring him in the face, sweet and hot and oh so easy to give in to. And that would be the end of everything. Orlando would kill him—no, that wasn't the way of it. Orlando would kill Jimmy and then commit suicide. Jonty's father would disown his son for having committed adultery, the fact he and Orlando weren't married being just a technicality. Then Mrs. Stewart would be the one to kill her son.

And for what? For a night's passion? Jonty was sure that Jimmy wouldn't be satisfied with a kiss or a cuddle, he'd persist in his chase until the ultimate prize was surrendered and colours struck. Perhaps the man really was looking for a permanent relationship as he'd hinted; he might well already understand that Jonty was rigorously monogamous. Maybe Jimmy genuinely wanted him to transfer that steadfast allegiance from Orlando to himself. Or perhaps he'd dump Jonty once he'd taken his prize.

Jonty sank under the water, as if in cleaning his face he could purify his thoughts with it. If he'd really met Jimmy out in the street, rather than just in a dream, would he have

127

succumbed so easily? Would a single dazzling smile have broken through all his defences and left him as helpless as a babe in the man's arms? Had Jimmy been absolutely right when he'd insinuated that Jonty wanted to dally, had always wanted to do so, just needed to loosen his resolve and give in?

He'd been convinced that he had the power within himself to keep turning the man down, but acting the *Macbeth* scene as husband and wife had been a complete mistake, leading to all kinds of second and third thoughts.

He didn't want to go to Jimmy; he knew that in his heart of hearts, but some part of his soul must be being tempted, sorely so, or else he wouldn't be having these wretched visions. He was grateful it was Sunday and it would take little to allow Orlando to be let off divine service. Jonty needed to be alone with his maker, if not with his thoughts—they were far too troubled to be a consoling companion.

He decided he'd go to the Abbey, hear the comfortable words spoken afresh, listen to the lessons and the sermon, hope that the collect would give him some insight into his condition. Then he would pray fervently that this would all pass, leaving him and his dearest love to be alone together, happy again. Perhaps in communion with his God, Jonty Stewart might at last find a way to overcome the greatest threat to his happiness he'd ever known.

As it turned out, Orlando insisted on coming with him to the service, no doubt believing it would make his lover incredibly happy for him to enter into the House of God willingly for once. He probably also wanted to keep Jonty sweet if any possibility existed of Jimmy hovering about ready to pounce, and if that meant going to church without the slightest fuss, then so be it.

Jonty was unnerved at the genuine enthusiasm on display

and wished that he was in a mood to enjoy having a willing Orlando at his side for once, not one who kept fiddling with the service book or making wild calculations about the dates of movable feasts. He assented to his lover's accompanying him with as much grace as he could muster, although he knew it would leave his original intention untenable. How could a man fall to his knees and safely talk to his maker with one of the main objects of his concern at his side? Orlando would only want to know why Jonty was so distressed, so in need of comfort and absolution.

So they attended communion together, and the private sojourn with God would have to be postponed until a later date.

📖

The Dowager Duchess of Castle Combe bore as little resemblance to Antonia Dewberry as Bath Buns to a rugby ball. Orlando had somehow expected, given the similarity in rank, that this woman might be like Mrs. Stewart, but in this he was sorely disappointed. The lady was only ten years or so older than Jonty's mother, yet seemed sere and disinterested rather than still full of the love of life. He wondered what set of circumstances had led to such a decline in her vitality, whether it was illness or disappointment or some form of melancholy.

Jonty had done his homework, having asked his mother whether she knew anything of the Weir family. She did, of course—he supposed there wasn't a noble family in the land that she couldn't provide some information about—and interesting stuff it had proved.

Mrs. Stewart had known the duchess since she was a girl, a young thing to whom the older woman had taken a shine. As she related it, the Weirs had never been reproductively robust, struggling from generation to generation on just a single heir and rarely a spare, having nearly extinguished itself on one occasion when the only child caught smallpox. The present holder of the title was in his fifties and on his third wife, none of whom had provided the necessary successor yet, though there had been allegedly no lack of trying, including some said to be the wrong side of the blanket. None of this had been presented as gossip, of course. Mrs. Stewart had simply stated the facts, although perhaps not in such crude terms, without judgemental comment.

The present generation of Weirs had been unusual in having two offspring in it, and indeed another who had died in infancy, and hopes had been high that Jeremy (born much later than his brother and very much cosseted) might have obliged where his elder brother could not. A terrible hunting accident twenty years previously had brought an end to all those hopes.

The fellows of St. Bride's hid their investigative personas behind the simple façade of a social call on the duchess and began the conversation by exchanging news about the happenings of the Stewarts and the Weirs, although the latter had been sadly bland and lacking in significance compared to the former. Jonty seemed particularly uncomfortable as he related the doings of his nieces and nephews, especially at the spark of pain in the duchess's eye, soon hidden, which accompanied his account.

When the appropriate moment came, Orlando spoke softly, recognising that he should take the lead in this encounter. "Your Grace, I realise this might cause distress to you, although I would ask your indulgence. It is true that we have been asked to call by Mrs. Stewart—" it was a fact, she had insisted that they pay a visit to an old friend, investigation or no, "—but we've another matter we would like to ask you about."

For all that the duchess appeared dried up, she'd

demonstrated every sign of a sharp mind and an incisive intelligence. That had shown itself time and time again in their conversation. Now she simply inclined her head and fixed Orlando with an eye which was suddenly keen. "And this matter is?"

"A suspicious death which happened some twenty-five years ago at the House of Sulis. A girl, one who might be described as no better than she should be. We've been asked to look into her murder, which is what old Dr. Buckner believed it was."

"I remember Dr. Buckner very well—not professionally, but socially. He came of very good stock, you know. His mother was one of the Howards."

Jonty nodded his head and Orlando followed suit. Many of their acquaintance seemed to take the measure of a person by the length of their pedigree and whether they could trace it back accurately to the days of the Conqueror. "So we understand." They didn't, of course, but it kept the lady sweet to say so.

"I don't suppose you are one of the Glamorgan Coppersmiths?" She turned to Orlando, who had the suspicion he was being led astray.

"Nothing so auspicious, I'm afraid. Merely the Kent Coppersmiths, who are really of no great consequence." He caught sight of Jonty's little smile and was heartened; at least there was one person in the world to whom he was of particular importance. "Did Dr. Buckner ever speak to you of this young lady's death?"

"Why should he?" The duchess almost bridled, then regained her composure. "I can assure you, Dr. Stewart, Dr. Coppersmith, that we would never have spoken upon such matters. I am not one for idle gossip."

"But this wouldn't have been a matter for tittle-tattle."

Jonty kept the pressure up. "He would have naturally felt that he had good cause to mention it. Given the circumstances."

"And pray to what circumstances do you allude?" The dowager fixed Jonty with an eagle eye which wouldn't have been outdone by either his mother or granddame.

"To the fact," Orlando swooped in, naturally colluding with his friend in tactics which might disorient the lady and cause her to let any secrets slip, "that your son was present that night. The night when the girl was murdered."

"My son? Gerald?"

"No, your younger son. Jeremy. Didn't you know he frequented the House of Sulis?" Jonty took his turn to fire a question.

"Of course I did. He often took the waters there, like many an entirely respectable lad. Your father and uncles were among them, back in the seventies." Her smile seemed genuinely fond in remembrance of those times.

"Why did you think we meant your elder son?" Orlando felt that there might be the tiniest glimmer of a breakthrough in this possible slip of the tongue. "Was he too a client of the baths?"

"On occasions. But I assumed you meant him simply because Jeremy is dead, and has been for some time, as I'm sure you know, Dr. Stewart."

"I do and I offer my condolences now, being too young to give them at the time. I know my mother would want to do so as well."

"She always was very gracious, young Helena Forster. And you have her smile—a very fortunate inheritance, indeed."

Orlando worried that they were being sidetracked again. "Did Jeremy ever mention that evening? The one when Dr.

Buckner had come home in such a rage and cleansed his temple?"

"Why should he have done? Was he supposed to have been there?"

"There's no supposed about it." Orlando decided they'd pussyfooted enough and he was convinced the duchess knew more than she was divulging. "There are plenty of witnesses both to the fact that he was there and to the even more shocking—for you, that is—fact that he'd been very fond of the girl."

"Who told you that? Brian Appleby, I'll warrant. Sorry, he calls himself *Father* Appleby now." A small point of colour had appeared in both of the duchess's cheeks.

"No, it wasn't him." Orlando didn't feel inclined to say just who it had been and was intrigued to hear the animosity with which Appleby's name had been spoken. It wasn't the first time they'd come across evidence of ill-will towards this man. "Why should you choose him, among all the others who might have spoken to us about your son?"

"Because I don't trust him, priest or not. He could easily have told you a dozen lies as far as I'm concerned." The lady sat back in her seat, as if her word on the man's character settled the matter without chance of argument.

"Why should he have chosen to lie? I assure you that the fact of your son's affection for this unfortunate girl is attested to by other people."

"Then Mr. Appleby has led them astray in their understanding as well. My son may have sown some wild oats, as any young man might, but he would never have sought to link himself with such a woman for more than a dalliance." The duchess stopped, again implying that the matter was beyond argument.

"And would your other son?" Orlando had been intrigued by the reference to the present duke. "Would he have linked himself to such a girl?"

"I doubt it. He was newly wed twenty-five years ago." The lady smiled, softening the lines of her face and resembling for the first time someone who might have consorted with the young Helena Forster; she had an animation and life about her which had been lacking before. Perhaps it was the reference to a happier time, when there had been hope of an heir.

Orlando recalled Jonty's words about the lilies and the child. "Your Grace, I have another few direct questions which I must ask. We are keen to find the origin of some lilies which have appeared on Sarah Carter's grave every year. I feel confident—" he didn't, but was becoming good at bluffing, "—that they're not from any of the florists in the city and have come from someone with an extensive, very efficient hothouse."

"I can't help you in that regard—I have no such glasshouses here. I would obtain similar blooms from Bristol should I require them, for example when providing them for the church at Easter." She waved her hand at the vases of chrysanthemums and roses which graced her drawing room. "As you can see, my taste runs to more autumnal colours. I have never particularly liked white blooms, as your mother would be able to verify." She smiled sweetly at Jonty, but the sweetness might be hiding a bitter aftertaste.

Jonty took a deep breath, like a bridge player preparing to lay down his final card. "You've been very patient with us, very helpful—could you bear to discuss one last thing?"

The duchess nodded her head graciously. For all her anger at Brian Appleby she hadn't forgotten the lessons of her breeding.

"I appreciate that this might prove painful to consider, but we've been told Sarah Carter was probably with child in the year before her murder and that, for whatever reason, the child was never born. Can you shed any light upon this?" He smiled as sweetly as he could manage; if the duchess was not melted, then Orlando certainly was and had to bury his nose in his notebook to hide his confusion.

"A child? I would add that to your list of things to discuss with Father Appleby, Dr. Stewart."

"Are you suggesting this man knows who the child's father was?" If Orlando had really been a greyhound in the slips, his nose would have been twitching and his tail curled ready for the trap to spring. "Or are you implying that Appleby himself sired the poor little mite?"

"I would rather say no more on the matter, not wanting to slander someone's allegedly good name." The duchess clenched her fingers tightly. "I don't mean to be obstructive, but this is a very difficult matter for me. Our line is a very old and influential one. We came over with the Conqueror, but we shall no doubt be extinguished in the days of the Saxe-Coburg-Gotha. I find all this talk of offspring both tasteless and inconsiderate, especially considering the provenance of the mother."

Orlando noted Jonty move forward then retreat, as if he'd been tempted to reach out and touch the woman's hand. He might well have done so for other of his mother's friends, but this lady had put up a barrier of reserve and the gesture wouldn't have been at all appropriate.

"Your Grace." Orlando's voice had fallen almost to a whisper. "Is there any possibility, however remote, that the child could have been your son's? And that he asked the girl to do away with it so as to preserve the reputation of your family?"

The duchess fixed Orlando with an eye which was so cold and suddenly reptilian that the man literally jumped in his seat.

"Dr. Stewart." She looked at Orlando but would not deign to address the man directly, something which made him extremely conscious of his misdemeanour. "Would you please make something clear to your friend? Families such as ours have a reputation above besmirching. And we do not take the law into our own hands." The duchess rose, and her guests naturally did the same. "I have nothing else to add."

Chapter Ten

"So it's a case of find the father, in more ways than one. Eh, Orlando?"

The fellows of St. Bride's had taken their notebooks into the hotel library, with the intention, or so Orlando thought, of looking at the case so far. But Jonty had refused point-blank, saying that they simply didn't have enough information at present, that they'd made many a false assumption on cases in the past because they'd jumped the gun, and anyway he wanted a long cool glass of lemonade before he applied his enormous brain to anything.

"Hm?" It seemed that Orlando's brain was equally in need of some lubrication.

"Brian Appleby. We need to find him and get his input. Not just because what he has to say might be valuable, but because he's the only one of the group who seems to have caused friction with the rest. I'd love to know why."

"We don't even know if he's still in the country."

"Oh, I bet he is, Orlando. The way the duchess talked about him for a start. She seemed fairly sure that we could catch up with him, and she didn't strike me as the sort of woman to get things too far wrong. Now, do you think he would be Roman Catholic?"

"Hm?"

"That seems to have turned into your word of choice. You're not becoming taciturn on me, are you?"

"Never in life." Orlando tried hard to look repentant. Jimmy was loquacious enough for ten and he didn't want to risk losing any ground against his opponent, even though things seemed to have turned rather quiet on that front the last few days. He only hoped the silence wasn't a guilty one. "I was just musing on denominations. Why do you think that Appleby's a Catholic? He could be Methodist or Unitarian for all we know."

"Well, of course. All I meant was that he has to be one of these fancy denominations or else Bredon could have looked him up in the latest Crockford's. Hold on." Jonty wandered over to one of the shelves and pulled down a book. "I mean, if he was good old Church of England we could just open this at Appleby and...oh."

"Why *oh*? What have you found?"

"Him, Orlando. He's in here—got a parish just outside Stroud, which is rather convenient. But that fact makes the mystery even deeper."

"What mystery?"

"Oh, you are being so obtuse. That's having all that Yorkshire pudding with your roast beef. Glutton. If he's so close and if he's listed in here, why didn't Bredon know where he was? Or was it a case that he knew and wouldn't admit? All very odd."

"We should try to get his number from the operator, then ring him and make an appointment for tomorrow." Orlando was at last starting to show signs of animation again, signs which had been sorely lacking after he'd sat down in the enormous, exceedingly comfortable chair.

"I bet his housekeeper doesn't approve of using the telephone on the Sabbath." Jonty grinned.

"Should we ring tomorrow then? It seems a shame to waste a day, but..."

"I'll ring. If she gives me any nonsense I shall remind her that the Sabbath was yesterday and today is the Lord's Day, what's left of it. I'd better be quick or he'll be off to evensong."

While he waited for his friend's return, Orlando mused on why Bredon might have lied, why the duchess hated Appleby so much and whether he had any room in his tummy for more than a light supper.

"Wake up!" A familiar voice broke into his reverie.

"Wasn't asleep. Just resting my eyes."

"Shame you couldn't rest your vocal chords at the same time. Sounded like someone was taking the pigs to market."

"Was your call successful? Did you make an appointment for us or did you just get Father Appleby's housekeeper to teach you a host of new insults?"

"Both. Only the appointment's just for you. I have work to do on that book, or else it'll never see light of day, then I have to persuade someone that he's playing a grand lady of passion and nerve rather than a debutante." Jonty assumed his most innocent and hardworking of looks.

Orlando's short sleep, or rest of the eyelids or whatever it was, had left him surprisingly refreshed and playful. He regretted that his lover wouldn't be at his side when he entered the fray, although he had an inkling that—for all his wild past—Appleby might be rather disapproving if he suspected that his two inquisitors were more than friends. So perhaps going solo was the best plan, even if it were arrived at by default. "I suppose you might actually have a harder prospect of it."

"I think you could be right." Jonty stretched. "Now, while you've got your wits back, I've another hare to get going. Talking to the housekeeper set me thinking—have you considered we might be chasing the wrong group of people? We've never considered the servants who were at the House of Sulis at the time."

"I have." Orlando ran his hands through his hair. "I was hoping we wouldn't have to pursue them—it'll be almost impossible to find out who they were and where they are now, seeing as Dr. Buckner didn't see fit to record that information."

"It's an interesting oversight. Perhaps it's one which should reassure us. If he had no reason to suspect the servants, we shouldn't, either."

"That seems a bit too glib. Maybe Buckner was just too trusting, as he'd been with the man who ran the baths while he was away."

"Well, I for one hope he got it right because it would be an awful lot of work, work we don't have time to do, if we need to go chasing them all after this time. Let's stick to what we have to hand, which for the meantime is Brian Appleby."

Jonty went to look for a railway timetable, to find the times of trains to Stroud. After a while they had a route planned, a strategy to assail their witness with and a slight rumbling in their stomachs to indicate that a light supper might just be due.

The supper was taken, along with an excellent bottle of Moselle, and a very mellow pair of academics made their way up the wooden hill to Bedfordshire.

"Still feeling tired, Orlando?" Jonty poked his lover's ribs as they entered their suite.

"Absolutely shattered. If you're planning the *let's fool the chambermaid by sleeping in the other bed for at least ten minutes* run, I'm afraid I can't be party to it." Orlando wore his 'sorry I'm such a failure' face, the one he'd come to Bath with and which he brought out a bit too often now.

"Ah, well. Can't be helped, I suppose." Jonty gave him a

kiss, trying hard not to let slip any sign that he wanted to make love tonight so he could be reminded he had Orlando in his bed and not Jimmy.

📖

Jonty meandered along the streets of Bath, pretending to look in shop windows. He'd anticipated a difficult Monday, just kicking his heels around the city, thinking of ways to avoid going to see Jimmy and equally convoluted ways of letting the man know.

He aimed a vicious kick at a stone, turned the corner and couldn't quite believe his luck. Coming towards him, not twenty yards away, was a potential partner in, if not quite crime, then a little bit of innocent mischief. "Miss Peters! Miss Peters!"

"Dr. Stewart, I did wonder if I'd see you here." Miss Peters grinned, emphasising wrinkles round her eyes and mouth that must have been earned by many a smile over the years. The sister of the Master of St. Bride's, she'd seen much more of the outside world than her distinguished brother. "How goes the work?"

"Fine, as far as we can see. Dr. Coppersmith is making great progress with his incunabula so today he's off playing Sergeant Cuff, which makes him happier than anything."

"And you? Not getting too bored?"

"No," Jonty replied, just a bit too quickly.

"By which you mean *yes* but you don't want to say so?" Miss Peters smiled shrewdly. "You're prevaricating, young man."

Jonty had the awful feeling she'd seen right through him. "Can't hide anything from you, can I? Are you free for a spot of lunch? I could use someone to talk to."

Miss Peters frowned, sticking out her bottom lip like a girl. "I can certainly make lunch, if it's an early one. If you need to talk now, I could delay my appointment for an hour..."

"No, I'll meet you afterwards. George's at noon, sharp, then?" The meeting was agreed to and Jonty wandered off, rather dazed at his own audacity. Why he'd started to expose his heart, even to the Master's sister, was beyond him. He had to take refuge in his work, cramming himself with Shakespeare and scribbling notes, until his mind was clearer.

They met at the restaurant and, while they waited for their meal, Jonty showed Miss Peters how his book was progressing, including all the amendments he'd made that very morning.

She nodded attentively, asked some pertinent questions, then admired the boldness and scope of the text. "So you just need that last little bit? I'm afraid I can't help you on that one— no trochophorian larvae in the Bard, as far as I'm aware."

"Trochophorian? You make up as many words as Shakespeare did." Jonty sighed. "I wish I could find something as simple as larvae in there—they might be a sight less difficult to put one's finger on than the rival poet, who is being particularly elusive. There must be more to it than just a competitor in both work and love."

"Why? You literary types are always looking at things so very deeply, finding meanings and hidden allusions that are probably never intended. I don't pretend to know the first thing about such matters but I'd say it was a plain case of jealousy, both on the work and romance front." Her face suddenly wrinkled up into a laugh that soon threatened to render her breathless. "Oh, listen to me sounding as if I actually knew what I was talking about. Come on, there's some seafood hoving into view and we'd best compose ourselves."

As they ate, the conversation turned to the reason for Miss

Peters's sudden appearance on the streets of the city like a guardian angel. It didn't seem to be the usual sort of thing an angel would be engaged in, looking for a microscope manufacturer. Although being there on behalf of her brother, who was laid up at Bride's recovering from a nasty fall, must have had some innate virtue. "And he wasn't drunk and staggering home from the Bishop's Cope, Dr. Stewart, his name's not Coppersmith."

Miss Peters had to admit that, although her quarry wasn't actually to be found in Bath but in Bristol—*that bloody place again,* Jonty thought—she hadn't been able to resist the opportunity of stopping off and trying to make contact with her two favourite fellows.

The chatter flowed on, touching on the gossip from Cambridge and gradually turning to Orlando's endeavours with his incunabula, their involvement with yet another murder mystery and Jonty's encounters with the Scottish Play.

"It's a shame I won't be here to see it open, especially if you do get to take the part of a tree." Miss Peters smiled insouciantly. "I would have cheered most heartily when you appeared and would have made no remarks about squirrels or their depredations."

"I do so wish you could come along. Do you have an hour this afternoon? We could go up and watch the rehearsals. I would so like you to meet Jimmy." Jonty came to a sudden halt, the silence speaking volumes.

"Jimmy? Is he one of the actors?" Miss Peters had no doubt picked up the strange quivering in Jonty's voice when the matter of the play had first been raised. She wouldn't need to dissect his brain nor lay out its neural networks to tell something was amiss or that this *Jimmy* was at the heart of it.

"No—well, yes, but he's also the manager of the company.

143

We knew each other some time ago, back at University College." Jonty pushed away his pudding uneaten, a sure sign for Miss Peters to read that things were indeed serious.

"Had you kept in touch?" Miss Peters seemed to be weighing each word carefully. "I suppose it was a pleasure seeing him again?"

"It was." Jonty sighed and fiddled with his food, none of it going onto his spoon or approaching his mouth. Things were going from bad to worse. "And it wasn't. Miss Peters, I trust I can speak to you in total confidence and not a word of this will get back to Orlando?" His eyes bore a look like a small child might employ on a confidante to inveigle him not to snitch to his parents.

"Now what sort of a girl do you think I am? Of course I wouldn't go blabbing. Dr. Stewart, whatever is the matter?"

"He attracts me." Jonty lowered his voice and addressed the battered remains of his trifle; he couldn't face looking straight into his guest's astute eyes, fearing he would find himself already condemned in their gaze. "He has made his way into my heart quite insidiously, being charming, kind and delightful. I don't love Orlando any the less, that's the strange thing, but Jimmy awakens all sorts of feelings in me. And he knows that he does."

"Would you let him kiss you? I'm sorry, that's the old maid in me talking—you know what I really mean."

"I hope not. I've vowed that I would never let it happen, as surely as if I'd spoken the marriage vows. But I can conceive of a situation in which that might come about."

Miss Peters lightly touched Jonty's arm. "Dr. Stewart, you've never struck me as being the roving type. You really value fidelity, don't you?"

"I do, above all things. I demand it as much of myself as I

do of others."

The lady smiled and shook her head. "Then why are we even having this conversation? You know what to do, or should I say what *not* to do. Make it so."

Jonty shut his eyes and took a huge breath. "I want to, so much, but you have no idea how hard that is. You've never met Jimmy Harding. He could charm the birds from the trees, the very stars from the sky. When he looks at me and says 'I know that you want to', I feel as if he's penetrating my very consciousness—I'm afraid that one day I'll just give in, irrespective of whether I would like to."

"Dr. Stewart. Jonty." The unprecedented use of his Christian name by Miss Peters made Jonty open his eyes again. "You know the verse about *if your hand offends you, cut it off.* I never took that to be literal, I think it's about your life. If Jimmy Harding tempts you, then don't see him again. As simple as that."

"But the play—we have to be in contact..."

"Then always have Dr. Coppersmith with you, at least in your mind's eye. And when this Jimmy looks at you, think of him. Remember where your priorities lie and do what has to be done." Miss Peters squeezed Jonty's hand. "I can easily find an hour or two this afternoon, if you would like a lady of a certain age to come up and watch the rehearsals. I shall sit there like an Old Testament prophetess acting as your very visible conscience. Perhaps this Jimmy—does he have a surname, as I couldn't be so bold as to address him by his Christian name?— will fall for a woman probably old enough to be his mother and I could whisk him away. That would solve every problem, wouldn't it?"

Jonty raised Miss Peters's hand to his lips and gently kissed it. "I can think of no eventuality that would make me happier." He picked up his spoon again and began to make his way through the poor, neglected trifle, which would have suggested to anyone who knew him that his mood was getting back to normal.

📖

"Good morning, I have an appointment with Father Appleby. Father Appleby is expecting me—please could you tell him that I am here? Here is my card—my colleague rang yesterday to arrange a meeting with Father Appleby."

As he walked up from the railway station to the rectory, Orlando worked through the possible variations on the introduction. He knew that first impressions were crucial and wanted to make the very best one on the housekeeper. He'd got the impression from Jonty that she was a bit of a dragon, and he didn't want to find himself cast in the role of sacrificial offering.

Inevitably, he found that he'd been led well and truly astray. The lady in question couldn't have been more charming and helpful, ushering him in to the rector's study, giving profuse apologies on his behalf that Appleby would be late, but there was a poor babe, born too soon and unlikely to see out the day, which he needed to baptise. She gave her guest tea (excellent) and biscuits (almost as good as Mrs. Ward's) and left him in the pleasant room to admire the view out to the garden.

Orlando wasn't a spiritual man—something Jonty regretted deeply—but as he sat in the little room and admired the sunshine on the lawn and flowers, he felt perhaps there might be something more to life than just murder mysteries, applied mathematics or even loving Jonty. Yet what it was seemed to be just around the corner, or slightly out of his sight, like a faint star that couldn't be seen if you looked at it straight on and would only be observed sideways, out of the corner of one's eye.

The rector arrived and all Orlando's thoughts returned to the murder.

"Dr. Coppersmith, I hope you will accept my most profuse apologies." Brian Appleby was a handsome man who reminded Orlando immediately of Dr. Peters; he had the same quiet authority and presence.

"There is no need to apologise. I couldn't come in the way of your duty." Orlando offered his hand and had it shaken warmly. Whatever had estranged this man from the duchess, it wasn't to do with his natural manner. He was utterly charming and sincere, or appeared to be.

"I appreciate your understanding—Mrs. Jordan explained the reason, I assume. I hasten to add that I feel no need to baptise children to assure their inclusion in heaven—I couldn't believe in a God who would cast out one of these little innocent ones. But it comforts the parents so much to perform the rite. I merely hope that in sixteen years' time the lad will still be alive and as strapping as a young oak. Ah, thank you." He took a cup of tea from the housekeeper, who had glided into the room and replenished their supplies. "Do you have children yourself, Doctor?"

"No, I'm a confirmed bachelor, I'm afraid, married only to my equations." Orlando smiled. "As you seem to be to your calling."

Appleby inclined his head. "Indeed, I've never found the woman who might tempt me from the straight and narrow. Now, to business. Your colleague, for I believe he was the one who called, said you wanted to ask some questions relating to a killing which happened some time ago."

"I do, indeed. Twenty-five years ago a girl died at the House of Sulis and the owner believed she'd been murdered." He watched for some reaction from the rector but all he received was a nod of the head and a studious look. "Do you recall such an incident?"

"I remember a girl, a prostitute, who died one evening after I had been visiting those baths with a party of friends. Is that the incident to which you refer?"

"It is. Do you recall her name?"

A small cloud of unease, or unhappiness, some negative emotion, crossed Appleby's face. "Sarah Carter. I could never forget her. I remember her death—we didn't hear of it at the time, we were keeping our heads down after being found in such a compromising situation. I heard a rumour that one of the girls had died and that an inquest was taking place. They said that her death was due to natural causes, but if Dr. Buckner believed there'd been foul play, then there might well have been. He was a very shrewd man."

"That's exactly what he believed, although he was too afraid to make such an accusation when she died. He felt guilty about the fact all his life."

"Men carry their burdens of guilt a long way, Dr. Coppersmith. I know that very well."

Orlando tried to work out if he was referring to personal or professional connotations but was left unable to decide. "I believe you sent flowers to the funeral."

"We did, a group of us—Bredon, Weir, myself. Again, we were too cowardly to attend in person. The tribute was some lovely hothouse blooms from the Weirs's Castle Combe estate, I think, or were they from Bristol? I really don't remember. Does that fact matter?"

"It might. Someone still leaves flowers on her grave, roses and lilies that seem to come from a glasshouse somewhere. It would be useful to know who still remembers the girl with such kindness."

Appleby smiled and shrugged. "Not me, I'm afraid. I haven't the facilities here to grow such things, and I've been out of the country on and off these past years. Although I'm glad someone makes remembrance. For all that she was a fallen woman, she was a lovely little thing. Very smart and such fun to be with. Her conversation was as important as..." He shook himself, as if in sudden realisation that he was straying down paths he shouldn't be treading.

"Did you know anything about her husband?"

The rector looked genuinely surprised. If he wasn't depicting his real feelings then he was a consummate actor. "A husband? I do think you're wrong there."

"We have been told the fact by more than one person."

"Then more than one person is wrong. Or perhaps..." Appleby considered for a moment, "...perhaps she lied to more than one person. Gave herself an imaginary husband as some sort of protection."

"Did she often tell lies?"

The rector shrugged again. "Those sorts of girls often do. Pretend that you're the one they like best—they tell that to every one of their gentlemen or so I understand. Perhaps lying becomes habitual."

"And why pretend she had a husband? How could that protect her?"

"It might stop any of her particular gentlemen getting too close or too possessive. Or it might be a threat she could use— 'Don't treat me badly or I'll tell my husband.'" Appleby spoke the last part in a stunning impersonation of a woman's voice, making Orlando wonder whether he had many Mary Magdalenes to deal with in his parish.

"And did you know about the baby?"

A silence struck the room like a bolt of lightning, cleaving the air and seeming to illuminate the rector's face. It was suddenly stony and grave, quite unlike the avuncular air it had worn all through the interview. "You know about the baby? How?"

"We were told by Thomas Critchley. He was absolutely sure about things."

When Appleby at last spoke, his voice was both tentative and subdued. "She told him? She swore that no one else knew."

Orlando realised that this news was causing the rector great distress and wished to soften the blow. He didn't often take that stance with male witnesses. "Maybe she told one of the other girls and *she* couldn't keep silent. However it happened, at least one other person knew, as surely as if she had told them directly."

"Dear God." Appleby didn't utter the phrase in a sacrilegious way, but like Jonty would speak it, a direct appeal to the Father he loved and trusted.

"Reverend Appleby, what can you tell me?"

The rector sighed. "Dr. Coppersmith, I have done a number of things in my life that I'm not proud of and which I've sought forgiveness for. One of the reasons I took Holy Orders was that I wanted to make amends for some of those things." He plucked a flower from the vase on his desk and began to fiddle with it. "That child was mine. She told me she was expecting and like an idiot, I pleaded with her to be rid of it. I was frightened for my name and reputation—I was a fool. She said she couldn't do such a thing, and I spent a fortnight in anguish, wondering how I could ever tell my parents. Then I received a message to meet her—she said she'd miscarried the child. It had happened just after we'd last spoken and she had been recovering in the interim."

"And did you believe her? That the loss of the child had been natural?"

"I did wonder, but she assured me time and again that it had been so. That didn't make my guilt any the less. Intention is just as bad as action in my book." He shook his head. "We remained friends, if such a thing can be said of a lady of pleasure and her patron, but things were never the same. I truly thought our secret had gone to the grave with her."

Chapter Eleven

"How was your day?" Orlando looked both tired and excited. He'd leaped up as Jonty entered the room to greet his lover in both words and gestures, a huge embrace with a tender kiss.

"Excellent, all in all, and this is just a perfect little cherry on the top, as my brother Clarence used to say when younger." Jonty returned the kiss, this time with a hint of real passion. "I had lunch with a lady."

"A lady? Who?"

"Miss Peters. She's off to Bristol—what is it about that place Orlando, we must go and see for ourselves—on her brother's business and I happened to bump into her."

"Is she still here? Have you asked her to dinner?" Ariadne Peters was one of the few women whom Orlando actually liked. The thought that she'd been swanning around nearby, and he hadn't got a look in, riled him.

"No, she had other fish to fry. I took her up to watch the play practice, though." Jonty hadn't trusted himself to meet Jimmy again but Miss Peters's idea of acting as a chaperone had worked perfectly. "You should have been there and seen her give Jimmy what for."

Orlando smiled at the thought. "I can imagine her belting the man about the head with her parasol or taking him over her knee and having at him with a slipper."

"Not quite, although she had just as powerful an effect. There she was, watching the rehearsals so demurely, but all the while she had Jimmy fixed with a penetrating look. Just like she was a Sunday school teacher trying to catch him out should he stray but a hair's breadth from the path of righteousness." Jonty chuckled. "I think he found it disconcerting. He's used to women flirting with him, whatever their age or standing, and to be the object of such intense moral scrutiny couldn't have been in his range of experience."

"Did it work? Did he behave himself?"

"Like a dream. He was on his best behaviour throughout. Almost." Jonty didn't mention that Jimmy had been flirting with both of them—that would have raked up old hurts and present temptations—nor that Jimmy had briefly put his arm round Jonty's shoulder. At least he'd immediately withdrawn his hand when Miss Peters muttered, "Don't touch what you can't afford," but Jonty wasn't quoting that, either. "I wish she could be there for the rest of the rehearsal period."

"That lady goes up in my opinion every time I have anything to do with her. The world would be a much better place if they let her and your mother run it. There'd be no wars—no one would dare start one—and there'd be no murders or the like."

"I'm not sure you'd actually welcome that latter eventuality, dearest. You got bored enough this summer without a felon to winkle out. How would you cope if all the mysteries went?"

"Ah, but they wouldn't. I've been thinking about it and if mysteries won't come to us, we'll have to go to them. Like turning our brains to solving who murdered the Princes in the Tower, or why and how Stonehenge was built. Or who your dark lady really was."

Jonty groaned. "Don't remind me. I've got almost all of this blessed book done now, except for the end. That dark lady and the rival poet are starting to give me nightmares." He stopped, having reminded himself of *that dream.* "So how was your little expedition? Did Father Appleby come up with the goods?"

"In spades, Jonty. Let's dress for dinner, then I can tell you all about it over a sherry or two." Orlando tapped his notebook significantly. "I think this time we can really get our teeth into things."

📖

"So where are we exactly?"

They were in the restaurant enjoying a light salad of shrimps and avocado in preparation for the main course of chicken in a white wine sauce, but that wasn't what Orlando meant. The post-mortem of the interviews had begun. He slid his notebook onto the table for reference, and a little pencil lay alongside it so he could make surreptitious notes, being furtive because he had the feeling this wasn't quite the done thing. Everyone would have called it bad form, discussing murder over a meal, let alone making objective notes about it. But they'd appropriated a table off to one side of the restaurant—not in a fashionable corner but near the kitchen door—where they could talk and not risk being overheard.

"We're at the stage where we have to be careful not to go haring off down blind alleys." Jonty scooped up the last of his shrimps and helped them down with a soupçon of Pouilly Fumé. "I remember when we made all sorts of assumptions about the Woodville Ward. I would be loath to be so foolhardy again."

"Then let's start with the bald facts and as we recite them

we can see whether a theorem will follow."

"You sound as if you're addressing your dunderheaded students."

"I'm sorry. Your mental acuity far exceeds that of any dunderhead I've ever known." Orlando grinned and slurped down a bit of Pouilly Fumé as well. Whatever other talents he possessed, and they were manifold, Jonty was also an excellent judge of wine, having been educated at his father's knee in choosing the right bottle to go with food. Not that Mr. Stewart was a wine snob—he swore that the best stuff he'd ever tasted was at a little roadside tavern in Normandy when he and Helena broke their honeymoon travels one day for a lunch of French bread, local tomatoes and goat's cheese. The wine had been served in little carafes, without label or vintage, and had tasted like nectar.

"Thank you." Jonty bowed his head in acknowledgement. "We have a dead girl who is said to have had a husband, although no one knows anything about him, even those who were—forgive me for the phrase—intimate with her at the time."

Orlando nodded. "And at some point before she died she was with child, Brian Appleby's child, and under duress to, well, make it otherwise." He stopped and took a deep breath. "I'm sorry, Jonty. It distresses me to talk about it."

"I know. Doesn't seem right at all, does it?"

Orlando shook his head, wishing he could lean over and take Jonty's hand, but that could never be done in such a setting. "And it's odd, because I don't mind talking about murder. Remember poor old Matthew's father? We talked of gruesome things then, yet this..."

"Indeed." Jonty smiled tenderly at his lover's kind-hearted nature, so often hidden behind the stern façade of his countenance. "Still, the child was no more, that's a simple fact and we don't know for sure whether that was a natural phenomenon. I'd say we should leave it at that, except for this business about the Weirs wanting to continue their line."

"Surely they wouldn't want a child who wasn't legitimate?" Orlando knew all about Henry VIII's bastard son being groomed for the throne but couldn't believe that the rest of the nobility would be quite so lackadaisical regarding the laws of inheritance.

"Maybe they'd have tried to find some way or another of managing to pass it off as the genuine article. We'll have to get Papa to give us the definitive answer about what's allowed. Until we know that..." Jonty shrugged. "What we do know is that someone remembers her with enough affection to send flowers. Expensive shop-bought or lovingly home-grown, it makes no odds but simply speaks of a degree of caring that's quite unexpected. It also implies resources that would make it out of the scope of her fellow fallen women, as Mama blessedly refers to them. Appleby says it isn't him and Jeremy Weir is dead. Actually, everyone denies that they send the flowers, so we're either missing a vital witness or someone is lying."

The waiter came to take their plates and Orlando was pleased at the short respite; he knew in which part of this investigation he'd been remiss. "I didn't ask everyone I spoke to about the flowers," he said eventually. "Someone might have been happy to admit to sending them, I just missed the chance."

"Perhaps. Anyway, there are other elements to consider. Like the fact that her clothes had been taken. I keep feeling that's at the heart of this case."

"You said that about the baby and the flowers."

"And I haven't changed my opinion. Let's think for a moment why anyone would take an armful of garments." Jonty tucked into his chicken, smiling at each well-seasoned mouthful.

"I assume she was only partly dressed when killed." Orlando pointed with his fork, something Mrs. Stewart would probably have given him another whack for.

"Why's that?"

"Because it's very difficult to get a dead body out of clothes. Don't splutter, it's not becoming." Orlando lowered his voice. "I have experience in this regard, admittedly not with a dead body but with you, once, when you came in from having dinner with your English colleagues. You flopped onto the sofa, totally out for the count, and I could hardly get your shoes off, let alone your jacket."

"Was that when I woke up freezing cold in the middle of the night and found the note pinned to me about *Don't try coming into my bed*? 'Strewth. No wonder it took me a bottle of best claret and a whole day of grovelling to gain re-admittance to that hallowed couch." Jonty grinned. "So she was dishabille before death. Then why should the killer go, find her clothes and take them?" The question was rhetorical. "I have a theory..."

"Out with it, then."

"I think it might be to do with leaving a trail of evidence. Perhaps those clothes had belonged originally to the killer's mother or sister, been thrown out, retrieved by said son or brother and then given to Sarah Carter in recognition of favours received. She'd have welcomed them, no doubt."

"And would they have been that easily traceable? Back to the lady who'd had them originally?"

"Quite possibly. If they were distinctive enough and if they'd been previously worn to some great event. People notice these sorts of things, particularly women. Someone might have seen the body and said *Isn't that dress the spit and image of the one Lady Velocipede wore to the Cheltenham races?* Then the cat would be among the pigeons. I think it entirely possible that all the men in Sarah Carter's party would have had access to cast-off clothes from some relative."

"You may have a point. It seems more likely than just taking them from plain spite, but then, when have we ever found a murderer who obeyed pure logic?"

"That never will happen until *you* take to it. Now let me finish this and we can look at your next point while we wait for pudding."

The plates were cleared away and a pair of apple tarts ordered. They referred to the notebook again.

"So," Orlando began, "I think there is little point in trying to play the alibis game and establishing who, in theory, couldn't have committed the deed. Far too far a remove."

"I agree with you entirely. Not that I'll ever have any truck with alibis—our last case completely vindicated me on that count. As far as I can see, just about anyone with enough nerve could have walked in and attacked the girl. Or anyone from inside, for that matter. It's like a rabbit warren in the House of Sulis now and I suspect it was worse back then."

"If not opportunity, then we must consider method. Strangulation seems relatively easy, especially if one can have some sort of an object in hand to help one."

Jonty rapped his lover's knuckles with his dessert spoon. "You've been listening to our police friends back in Cambridge with their gruesome tales of ties and necklaces again."

"I think the necklace idea is a valid one. I have a theory to put to *you* this time." Orlando paused to allow the apple tart to arrive and insinuate its aroma into his nostrils. "I think the killer must have gained the girl's trust. I can't be sure that she didn't put up a fight or make a din, but we could assume that it was probable, given that no one realised a death had occurred until the next day."

"Making assumptions is the dangerous sort of thing that dunderheads do but I'll allow it this time. We have no evidence either way."

"I was thinking about this on the train back here this afternoon. I imagined that I had to strangle you and not end up severely injured in the process." Orlando hid his grin with a spoonful of custard.

"Do you plan this sort of thing often? Murdering me, I mean. I suppose it's to get your hands on my money, then fulfil your dream of making some mathematical equivalent to the Nobel Prize."

"I could cheerfully devise a means of doing away with you when you insist on blethering like that." Orlando reached under the table, found Jonty's knee and pinched it, just above the patella where it smarted like stink. "This speculation was in the pure interests of our investigation. My conclusion was that if I approached you from the front and put my hands around your neck, then you would shout for Mrs. Ward and lump me one, both at the same time. I decided that I would have to do one of two things. I would have to be all lovey-dovey and sidle up, keeping you sweet all the while, then I might kiss your neck or some such thing and caress your shoulders. While you were— quite naturally given that it's me—ecstatic, I would tighten my grip and *voilà!*"

"I shall be very wary when you kiss my neck in future. I'll have some sort of an iron collar made as protection. What was the second stratagem?"

"I would buy you some lovely little gewgaw—a nice heavy piece, not delicate like your crucifix. I would murmur sweet imprecations and put it around your neck, then pull very hard. I think that might be an even more effective way to do things than with one's bare hands."

"I think you might be onto something there. It would put the girl at ease, the appearance of some little necklace, all twinkling gems and a heavy chain to hang them on. Mother has one or two pieces which would be eminently suitable augments to strangulation." Jonty finished the end of his apple pie, spooning up the little soupçon of custard which he always kept to last for a special treat. "And it would suggest that the killer was one of her paramours."

"Or the errant husband home from sea or wherever he'd been."

"I don't believe there ever was a husband, although I might be completely wrong—I think he was just a story someone put about. And even if he did exist I can't see him being full of joy and ready to give presents when he'd caught his wife almost *in flagrante delicto*. Still, we have a possible means. Now we just need a motive."

"Let's consider the ones we've come across before. Revenge upon a type—could it have been someone who disapproves of prostitutes and wants to kill them?" Orlando had his beloved notebook to hand. It amused him to see Jonty straining to read it from across the table, spectacles in prime position and all.

"Then there would have been more victims and there don't seem to have been. Vengeance for a particular affront seems more likely, which is why the killing stopped at one."

"And the affront? The killing of the baby? The besmirching of a family name? Having relations with one's fiancé?" Orlando tapped each idea on the paper as he read it out. "I can just about imagine Jeremy Weir's intended, if he had one, not liking his associating with loose women and wanting to kill the one who'd sullied him. But it seems very farfetched."

"Jealousy is a possible motive, you know. A girlfriend or even a sister might want to sort out the woman who was consorting with her man, although that does seem stretching it a bit. And we're getting along the lines of assuming that the killer is a woman. I can't see a father or brother taking that sort of revenge."

"Come on, let's rouse out some coffee. I have an idea or two to discuss."

Orlando rose from the table and escorted his friend in his best mannered style. He may not have been born with blue blood, like his lover, but he didn't want any disparity in their status to be obvious. When they'd been served a pot of the excellent brew which the hotel concocted, Orlando poured himself a cup then sat back.

"That's not good enough, you know. You should fill my cup, too." Jonty pointed at the coffee. "If two people pour from the same pot, one of them will have ginger twins before the year is out. That's what our old cook says."

"That woman might make the best pastry I've ever tasted but her wisdom is sorely lacking. You could never have those twins—there's no ginger hair in your family. Which brings us quite neatly to my theory. Brian Appleby, for all that he seems a delightful man and an excellent priest, is racked with guilt. He says it's over the baby and the fact that he might have been the cause of its death, but what if he was the cause of Sarah Carter's death, too?"

"That might drive any man to examine his faith." Jonty looked suddenly serious, as he always did when they touched on guilt and absolution. "He would find forgiveness, at some point, and he could feel he was making amends by his many good works. I have no doubt that he does good deeds,

161

Orlando—a penitent murderer could end up being a great credit to society, I would say. But I don't understand what motive he would have had to kill her."

"That Sarah Carter wouldn't marry him. I think he asked her to and she told him about her husband, despite what he said. Then she fell pregnant and he asked her to be rid of the child as it would both ruin him and bring her down in the eyes of her spouse."

"But why go so far as to kill her? And why so long afterwards? It makes no sense."

"Because, as you so astutely pointed out, she wasn't actually married. She just put the tale about for some reason, perhaps because she simply didn't want to marry Appleby and she found it the easiest way of refusing him. When he discovered she'd been lying..." Orlando waved his coffee spoon as if conducting an orchestra of facts, all of which were blending their tones to produce a theory.

"He took his revenge at the affront. It's possible, more than possible." Jonty's wonderful smile seemed to light up the lounge.

Orlando thanked heaven, once again, that the smile was reserved for him alone. "Now, what if Weir wanted to marry her as well, despite her social status? Appleby might have felt that he was a serious rival and, if he couldn't have her, no one could."

Jonty poured himself another cup of coffee, the threat of ginger twins notwithstanding. "I like this idea—let's turn it around a bit. If we assume both Weir and Appleby wanted to marry the girl and she was using the 'already wed' story to keep one or both of them at bay, isn't it possible that our friend Jeremy Weir might have murdered her? Because he didn't want Appleby going off with her and him not getting a look-in any more? I can imagine that they'd all be happy to share those girls' favours but be less than pleased if one of them was given exclusive rights. I'm sorry, I know this makes you feel uncomfortable, every time we get to the nub of what those girls were actually doing."

"It does—" Orlando shook his head, "—but I've got to accept that it happens, whether I like it or not. You're right about turning the theory round, it would still work. And those flowers could have come from the hothouses at Castle Combe—Appleby told me they have them there. The Weirs seem a strange family, what little I've seen or heard of them, and it wouldn't surprise me if Jeremy felt some peculiar mixture of guilt and love which made him want to remember his victim in a very public way."

"But you're forgetting something, Orlando." Jonty smiled again, like a delinquent angel. "Jeremy's dead, and, unless he passed the obligation onto Gerald, the sending of the flowers would have died with him."

📖

Tuesday morning Jonty woke early, the combination of morning sunshine and a particularly persistent blackbird proving fatal to sleep. He settled for watching Orlando gently slumbering, chest rising and falling almost imperceptibly— asleep, he looked very young and vulnerable. The thought that he'd been tempted, was still tempted, to threaten their love stabbed at his heart like a dagger. In the same way that Lady Macbeth's dagger of ambition had furthered her husband's position and so wrought destruction on them both, Jonty's desire for Jimmy threatened to destroy the very precious bond that lay between him and his true love.

He liked to think his mind was made up now, that there

was now no way in which he would succumb to Jimmy, whatever it cost him. But that wasn't the truth. It couldn't be, when his first waking thought these last few days had been about Jimmy and not Orlando. When he kept thinking about how the man smiled and laughed and what it felt like with his arm around your shoulder. He could put on an act with Orlando, be the usual impish Jonty, but he couldn't deceive himself.

He'd told Jimmy he wouldn't attend Tuesday's rehearsals because he would be working on his book, which was almost the truth. Jonty felt if he could only spend a few more hours alone with the rival poet then he'd hit the nub of things and he was determined to do it while Orlando was evaluating one of the remaining manuscripts.

Then they would go, together, and see Critchley in the afternoon, armed with a theory which they could test out. The man would likely prove more forthcoming than Gibbs the solicitor who'd seemed basically honest and incredibly dull. They wanted someone who might be inclined to embroider the truth but who was sufficiently a gossip to allow indiscretions to be committed. Whatever information they acquired could then be calibrated by putting the same points to Bredon.

And absorption in the puzzle would keep his mind from other things.

As it turned out, the morning went better than expected, Jonty suddenly finding three possible suspects on the rival poet front, all springing from his noddle like Athena from Zeus's cranium. He made a draft for the end chapter and was so pleased with himself that he went to the river and annoyed the ducks until the time came to meet Orlando at the station.

They went to Bradford on Avon for lunch, Orlando in as good a humour as his lover was, a humour that couldn't be diminished even at the thought of Critchley's inadequacies in the provision-of-tea department. They were expected, Jonty having phoned ahead, and, it being too early in their host's estimation to be offered the cup that cheers, were presented with a sherry that proved surprisingly drinkable.

"Dr. Stewart, I didn't expect to see you again so soon."

"We've gained some new information and would like to have it corroborated by a reliable witness." Jonty elaborately opened his notepad in an effort to hide the obvious lie. "When last we met you told me of Sarah Carter's baby. Who told you about it?"

"As I told you before, and I believe you made a note of it, Brian Appleby informed me."

"I did make a note but it contradicts something we've been told, therefore I wished to make sure I'd recorded you aright. I also asked if you knew who the father was and you said you didn't. Have you reconsidered that point at all?"

Critchley produced a crooked smile. "Dr. Stewart, you have a particular glint in your eye which reminds me of your mother. It could pierce a man at five yards. I have reconsidered and I still do not know."

"Sarah didn't tell you?"

Jonty was glad Orlando had asked the question; alternating the interlocutor had worked a treat, in the past, at loosening the tongues of their witnesses.

"Why should she tell me?" Critchley seemed undeterred by being interrogated.

"Because, as we understand it, it was she who told you about the baby in the first place, not Appleby." Orlando carried on the inquisition.

"Now there you are mistaken. I didn't find out until after her death, so she couldn't have told me." Critchley sipped his sherry demurely.

"Did you discuss this with anyone else after the inquest, or only with Appleby?" Jonty took up the baton.

"Am I supposed to have done? Can you imagine me sailing up to the duchess and saying, 'Your Grace, I believe your son got a prostitute with child and she got rid of the poor little thing'?" The colour rose in Critchley's cheeks, a pleasing sight on a witness as it normally meant they were onto something.

"So you believed the child's father was Jeremy Weir?" Jonty leaned forward, almost touching Critchley's knee.

"Of course not, I just used that as an example." Critchley pulled back, visibly shaken. "Anyone could have been its sire, any of the five of us there that night and who knows how many more."

"Did you ever mention it to Her Grace?"

Critchley fiddled with his glass. "Again I ask you, am I supposed to have?"

Orlando had clearly decided he should draw a bow at a venture, as they'd successfully done in the past. "Yes. Or so the lady avers."

Critchley placed his glass on the table with geometric precision. "I had wished to spare the duchess's blushes, but now I see that it's too late. I will tell all. We were at a soiree, some months after Sarah Carter died, and someone made an unfortunate remark about Brian Appleby considering taking Holy Orders. They alleged it was due to a theft he'd committed and now regretted. The duchess knew we'd all been friends and asked me why I thought he'd chosen such an uncharacteristic course."

"And you told her what, exactly?"

"That Appleby and I were no longer on speaking terms so I

couldn't possibly say what was on his conscience, except that he bore a burden of guilt over the girl who had died, possibly due to the matter of paternity. And that is a summary of the entire conversation."

"Just why did you become estranged from Appleby?"

"Because he began to air the possibility that the girl had been murdered and suggested we have the matter investigated. I managed to dissuade him—the scandal could not have been borne—and he agreed, at last, to keep his concerns to himself. But we never spoke again."

📖

"Who do you believe, Jonty?" They were making their way back to the station, heads whirring with new information and equally new uncertainties. "Which do you think is lying, Critchley or Appleby?"

Jonty shook his head. "I'm at a loss, truly. Here's a case of a girl whom everyone speaks highly of, yet who was brutally murdered. Everyone wanted it all covered up at the time but is quite happy to discuss all the details now. I can't even follow a thread clearly over who said what, to whom and when, nor even who lay with who."

Orlando briefly clasped his friend's arm. "It's a muddle but we'll sort it, we always do. Still, answer my question. What does your famous instinct tell you?"

"It tells me nothing, although I can relate what mother always used to say about our Mr. Critchley."

"Which is?"

"She wouldn't touch with a barge pole and she wouldn't trust him with a balloon on a stick."

Chapter Twelve

"You're not enjoying yourself, are you?" They'd come straight from the station to the House of Sulis to enjoy the waters before dinner, but the magic had gone, somehow. "There's not the usual Coppersmith enthusiasm for a warm soak."

Orlando shook his tousled head. "It's all changed, Jonty. When we first came here it was so delightful, all the marble and the mosaics and the peaceful atmosphere. Yet now all I can think of is what went on here twenty-five years ago—not just the murder, but the debauchery. It makes me feel unclean."

"Well, these things have gone on for thousands of years. There are prostitutes in the Bible, male and female. As long men and women have had something to barter with, some food or a nice animal pelt, they've sold their bodies for pleasure. And it will continue for as long as those conditions persist."

"It's not right. It's not about love and if it's not about love than what's the point of..." Orlando stopped short of saying the word *sex*. They may have been alone in the bath but he was taking no chances. "The point of *it?* Relations, you know."

"If only everyone had your enlightened outlook then the world would be a better place. But for some people *it's* just about pleasure or domination or animal lust or a million other things."

"Well, it shouldn't be." Orlando made the pronouncement as if he were ending a supervision on trigonometry and was telling the dunderheads they could make no argument against his declaration. Maybe he was telling Jonty to forget about Jimmy Harding, while he was at it.

"How about your Dr. Keane, then? He indulged in these sorts of things yet you still respect him."

"That's different. He was very kind to me and, irrespective of whether I approved of his—" Orlando tried to think of another word for *whoring* but drew a blank, "—activities, I admired his qualities as a man."

Jonty slapped his lover's shoulder. "You amaze me. We'll make a Christian of you yet. Come on, you look tired. We'll get dressed, have dinner and make an early night of it."

Orlando tried not to sound too hopeful. "What sort of an *early night* did you have in mind?"

Jonty was half out of the water, reaching for a towel to dry his highly attractive frame. Even more alluring, now it was dripping wet. "I did think of just sleeping, as you seemed rather low." There was something uncomfortable in his voice, a hint of reserve or of things being hidden.

Orlando bit his tongue. Maybe he was being punished for not having wanted to sleep with Jonty last time it was suggested; maybe it was something worse. However much he wanted to say, "you'll make love to me tonight and I'll not take no for an answer", that could never be said. "Perhaps that's for the best. You'll want all your wits about you when you talk to Bredon."

Everything else was left unspoken and remained so over a rather prickly dinner.

Derek Bredon was most apologetic that he was late for his eleven o'clock appointment with Jonty. He explained how he'd been with his man of business discussing various properties and matters had run on a bit. "However, I can promise you an excellent cup of coffee in recompense. I have it imported from America and it is without parallel in England or so I believe."

Jonty had been sceptical of the promise of said brew—he still had unpleasant memories of Critchley's hospitality, although the man had redeemed himself with his sherry the day before. But he was pleasantly surprised when the coffee arrived, its quality exceeding even that which Mrs. Ward produced, a thing he hadn't thought possible.

"Now, Dr. Stewart. Are you and Dr. Coppersmith any further forward in solving this mystery?"

Jonty sighed. "To be honest, Mr. Bredon, I feel like this case resembles that wretched maze at Hampton Court. We make progress, we establish facts, we think the solution keeps appearing just over the hedge and we hope we're nearly there. Then we discover we've gone down a dead end and we're no nearer than we were days ago."

"And do you hope that I'll be able to guide you through this labyrinth to the centre?" Bredon steepled his fingers, resembling some fellow in St. Bride's Senior Common Room discussing an abstruse theorem, not an all-too-real, violent death.

"That would be the most gratifying eventuality, yet we would settle for simply blocking off some of those dead ends and blind alleys."

"I will try my best, as I promised your colleague."

Jonty nodded, trying hard to retain a vestige of hope that they'd solve this baffling case. "I think you are unique in our experience, Mr. Bredon. Everyone else we've spoken to, while quite happy to discuss the past, has effectively cut themselves off from it. Only you seem to have bothered to keep in contact with those ladies, the ones with whom you were all so friendly."

Bredon shook his head. "It grieves me that we went to ground so completely at the time. None of us were brave enough to stand up and say that we'd been present that night or demand a proper enquiry into events. Now, for most of us, it's a stage of our lives which we look back on with a degree of something that almost resembles bravado. I suppose you've heard no end of talk about *sowing one's wild oats* and *a young man's fancy*, but people forget that those girls were real human beings, not lumps of meat to be used and discarded."

"But you didn't deny your past—you kept in touch with Clarissa up until her death. I believe that took quite a lot of courage." Jonty could only imagine the condemnation such a course might bring.

"As I told Dr. Coppersmith, she was very special to me. A friend rather than just a doxy." Bredon put down his cup and studied it.

Jonty felt he wasn't even beginning to scratch the surface with this man—however was he going to access whatever Bredon had kept from Orlando? "I've no doubt she appreciated the fact that you still went to visit her."

"And I appreciated that she would still receive me."

"She spoke to you about Sarah? I understand from Dr. Coppersmith she told you about that lady's husband and child."

Bredon stared into the distance, as if transporting himself back into the little set of rooms where Clarissa had lived. "She refused to talk about Sarah's death for years. She was scared, I think, to dig up old troubles. She didn't open her heart to me until she knew she was dying."

"What had frightened her?" Jonty opened his notebook, hopefully.

"The notion that whoever had killed Sarah was still alive and might come to find *her* if she stirred things. When Clarissa was at death's door it made no difference to tell what she knew."

Jonty could feel a strange stillness in the air, as if the shades of the dead girls hung about it, urging their champion on to discover the truth. "So she had clear suspicions about who'd committed the murder?"

Bredon nodded. "But she refused to share them with me. She said she might have been wrong and didn't want to get me into trouble. She would stick to sharing what she knew about Sarah and what she suspected. The rest was up to me and I'm afraid I didn't pursue things as I should have."

"She gave no impression of who she suspected? Could it have been the other girl, Adelaide?"

"Not her, I'm sure. When last I talked with Clarissa she'd recently heard from Adelaide, a long letter from Paris. Clarissa had only kind words for her old friend. I hope she had as kind words for me." Bredon passed his hand before his eyes. "Now, what have you to tell me?"

Jonty tapped his notes, a gesture which was becoming habitual for both him and his partner in investigation. "Well, we have four key features we think are crucial to the solution. The first are the flowers which are still sent to Miss Carter's grave. No one we've asked will admit to sending them."

"I can reassure you it's not me—we sent the tribute to her funeral and that's all."

"Might I ask where *those* flowers came from?" Jonty was hopeful at least one mystery might be solved, but in this he was again frustrated.

"Do you have a suspicion?"

Jonty eyed Bredon with a sudden perception of the truth; this man was, he believed, fundamentally honest, but unwilling to give anything away which hadn't been earned. "I think they came from the Castle Combe estate, from Gerald."

Bredon nodded. "That's a point to you. They did indeed, provided on the quiet by Jeremy's brother. We didn't wish to use one of the local florists and provoke suspicion."

"Might those hothouses still be providing tributes?"

Bredon shrugged. "Possibly, although I can't say under whose auspices. Jeremy has been dead a long time and I don't think Gerald knew the girl. He took his pleasures further away from home."

Jonty noted the points in his little notebook, although more for show than efficiency. "Now we come to our next point. Can you remember what Sarah was wearing the night she died? I mean, what clothes did she arrive at the baths in?"

Bredon seemed surprised by the question. "I don't remember. She always dressed very soberly, almost modestly—as did Miss Simmonds—which is more than can be said for the other girls present that night."

"Might they have been something which one of her gentlemen friends had given her? Did she dress in the sort of clothes that perhaps were outside her means to buy?"

"Now that you come to mention it, there had been occasions upon which both she and Clarissa had been very smartly turned out. We went to the races once, like a very decent party, and the third girl—I can't recall her name—had been rather put out at the cut of their cloth. Why do you ask?"

"Because the girl was found dead in only her underclothes and her outer garments were never accounted for. If they were deliberately taken then it might have been in an effort to cover up who'd bought or provided them."

Bredon smiled. "I see that you're obviously more efficient at your job than I gave you credit for, aren't you? I apologise here and now for underestimating your skills. *Amateurs,* I thought the first time I met your colleague, *liable to dig in, muddy the waters and leave the situation worse than it was.* That's why I was reluctant to be entirely frank before. I'll make amends for that now."

"I thank you on both counts." Jonty heard the pompous sound of his own voice then grinned. "Dr. Coppersmith will be most put out when I pass on your remarks, although it will be worth it just to see his face. Now, our third matter is the supposed existence of a husband. Did Clarissa have anything to say on this point? I've been led to believe that she was perhaps a bit...enigmatic...when she mentioned him."

"She was indeed. I suspect you've guessed why."

"Because he didn't exist." Jonty's eyes twinkled. The matter was becoming clearer as they spoke, half-formed conclusions now seeming like certainties. "That's why Clarissa gave a rueful smile to Mrs. Whats-her-name when she referred to the husband. She was in on the subterfuge."

"None of us knew at the time, honestly. Sarah had initially made up the story of a husband who might return at any moment from sea to protect herself when she worked in Bristol. Not just because he was a potential physical threat but because he helped keep at bay a particularly ardent old gentleman who wished to make an honest woman of her. When she set her sights on higher things and came to Bath, she kept up the subterfuge. At least on occasions."

"Then why did you suggest to Dr. Coppersmith that we go in pursuit of the husband, if you knew the story was all as sham as Ralph Allen's castle?"

"I'm ashamed to say I was testing your mettle. I wanted to see if you could work out for yourselves that the man didn't exist."

"It wasn't a deliberate attempt to put us off the scent? To protect an old friend, or even yourself?"

"Touché, Dr. Stewart. No, I assure you I would rather see Sarah's killer brought to book, if only for Clarissa's sake. I'm sorry if my remark caused you to turn down one of those dead ends, but I had to be sure. Those wretched stories of Conan Doyle's have put the idea of sleuthing into one or two heads where it should never have been inserted."

"Our mettle was beyond that level of testing." Jonty smiled, happily—he didn't mind his competencies being analysed. "We would never have sought to pursue the man, simply because we'd nothing to go on except the rumour that he was a sailor. If we'd eliminated all other possibilities, then perhaps we might have raised the hue and cry."

"And what have your investigations led you to conclude?"

"That Jeremy Weir wanted to marry Sarah Carter, but couldn't, because he believed she was already taken. Did she dislike him so much that she'd turn down the possibility of marrying into such a distinguished family?"

"I don't know if it was so much a dislike of him as affection for another person. She had hopes in another direction, if you follow me. However, I reiterate, I only found this out a few years ago. I had no idea at the time."

"And that affection was for the father of her child? Brian Appleby?"

Bredon smiled again. "Dr. Stewart, you've established much more than I expected, to winkle out such confidences. Yes, she'd set her cap at Appleby."

"Could she be sure that he actually was the father? We

175

know what her life involved—surely there must have been some degree of uncertainty?"

Bredon looked rueful. "She'd told Clarissa that due to the timings and circumstances, it could only be Appleby. Clarissa remained unconvinced."

"And so Sarah confronted the man she loved. What did Clarissa have to say on that point?"

"Two things. One would be the bare recital of facts, the other her opinion. Sarah told Appleby that she was expecting his child."

"And he panicked and asked her to be rid of it. That must have upset her enormously."

"Not according to Clarissa. She said she was surprised at Sarah's reaction—annoyed, peeved, but not distraught."

Jonty felt as if an unexpected light was starting to dawn. "Now, I wonder if that was because the child actually had another father? That she'd simply chanced her arm with Appleby, hoping it would force his hand into proposing marriage. If that failed, she knew she always had another place to turn."

Bredon grinned—a strange expression, less humorous than ironic. "I think you have Sarah's intention very well judged, although not the reality. While Clarissa had no evidence, she believed there never was a child."

"Dear God…" Jonty laid down his notebook, truly stunned. Everyone had spoken so well of Sarah Carter, she had been held in such affection, and yet it now seemed that she was simply a liar. An habitual liar.

"I'll tell the whole tale as Clarissa believed it." Bredon steepled his hands again. "Sarah was desperate to marry Appleby. Ironically, he showed no inclination to settling down with anyone and Jeremy Weir was the one interested, much to

Sarah's chagrin. So she drew a bow at a venture, told Appleby she was pregnant and hoped he'd offer to make an honest woman of her. He reacted in a totally unexpected way, so she waited a while then made up another story—that the nonexistent child had been lost, hoping her loss might make him fonder towards her."

"When Appleby met her again, and was told the child was lost, was he any more conciliatory?" Jonty sought to grasp this case afresh, make some sort of sense of the tangled knot of truth, supposition and downright lies.

"He was, but not to the extent she hoped. He'd offered to support the child, but he didn't propose having the banns read."

"Yet they remained friends, of a sort. He was still her..." Jonty searched for the right word for the man who used a prostitute, but gave up.

"Yes. I suspect that she'd never stopped carrying a torch for him. He, however, felt he couldn't entirely trust her, as has been shown to be true."

"He thought no one else knew about that child. And I suspect knowing he might have been the cause of its death has haunted him for years." Jonty shut his notebook; he wished to write no more.

"Sarah told Clarissa about it, I wouldn't be surprised if the word spread." Bredon folded his hands again, his story told.

They sat in silence for a few moments before Jonty took his leave, reflecting on deep emotions—trust, honesty, manipulation. For so long Sarah Carter had appeared to be a totally innocent victim. Now the case was turned upside down.

📖

"Well you've got plenty to get your teeth into there." Jonty, back in their suite, had given Orlando a blow-by-blow account of his most recent interview. "By the time I get back from the folly you'll have no doubt got it all solved. Then we can go down to the House of Sulis and you can stun me with your natural genius."

Orlando was still fuming at being regarded as a muddling amateur and equally surprised by the story according to Clarissa. "I don't think I ever want to go to those baths again. But don't let me stop you," he added hastily, knowing how much Jonty enjoyed soaking in the hot waters and not wanting to spoil his fun.

"Would you mind if I took a soak en route home? I feel the need of unwinding—I've had one or two surprises too many this morning." Jonty shuddered.

"And what are you up to this afternoon? Lady Macbeth still playing up?" Orlando felt less than comfortable about his lover being in the treacherous vicinity of Jimmy Harding but there was little he could do short of placing Jonty under curfew.

"Ah, now, her ladyship has made great strides. He—she—it—oh, you know, no longer sounds as if she's calling the cattle home o'er the sands of Dee. Although the lesser actors are playing up a bit and I'm under severe pressure again to be a tree. Birnham Wood are an absolute shower and Jimmy feels they need a bit of leadership."

Orlando rolled his eyes at the mention of the director. The man had been singularly absent from conversation of late and just as well; he still wanted to land a hefty one on his hooter. "Well, perhaps that would be a good idea. Jimmy's no great example to anyone. And," Orlando added with just a trace of cattiness, "he's hardly the type to be portraying some lithe young sapling. Distinctly tubby around the girth."

Jonty grinned. "Too much sticky toffee pudding, he says—he intends to work hard and sweat it all off. Not like you, Orlando. Not a spare ounce of fat on your tummy." He poked a finger into his lover's ribs and then rose from the table. "We part till dinner, Sherlock. Do have the solution ready for me. And not a seven per cent one," he added over his shoulder.

Jonty slid into the waters with a great sigh. It had been a long day among a week or so of long days. The House of Sulis provided a refuge where he could think and be at ease without fear of interruption, and at last he could have a chat with his maker about the temptations he was undergoing. The lure felt slightly more distant, especially when Jimmy wasn't within sight or sound. And when Jimmy had last been close by, the delivering angel Jonty had prayed for manifested itself as a woman of mature years—in a sensible costume and a ridiculous hat—and guarded his virtue. He wished he had Miss Peters by him to wield her sword of righteousness the rest of the time.

"Jonty." A voice floated up behind him. At first he thought it was just part of his thoughts, then realised this really was Jimmy himself. "I thought you'd stopped coming here. Every time I drop by you're notable by your absence."

Jonty turned, determined to face his pursuer—he didn't want the back of his neck attacked again, thank you. "Orlando rather feels the place has been sullied by associations with the murder that was committed here. And all other sorts of goings-on, it turns out." He looked down, wishing he'd had the sense to keep his gob shut and not make the sort of statements that Jimmy was bound to take and twist to make provocative.

"Perhaps I shouldn't ask about the exact nature of these

scandalous occurrences, discretion being the best part of valour. I love being gallant." Jimmy grinned, wonderfully handsome in the watery light. "So *he's* not here?" He eased himself into the water at his friend's side.

Jonty had forgotten what a fine body Jimmy possessed. They'd once shared a dressing room for an amateur production of *Twelfth Night* and he'd been privy to the sight of it several nights running. Jimmy had put on a bit of weight since then, but was none the worse for that, his frame having filled out into gently muscular curves. Jonty swallowed hard, trying to keep his gaze above the waterline so he couldn't see if Jimmy had filled out in other places, too. "Orlando's back at the hotel in the process of, I hope, clearing up the mystery."

"He won't want to be disturbed for a while, then." Jimmy closed his eyes and smiled. In the twinkling reflection from the water, the light that broke and danced over them, he looked stunning, the curve of his lips and glistening shoulders more alluring seen here than in the bright summer sun. "This is very pleasant. I hope you're not in as much of a hurry to leave as you usually are?"

Jonty couldn't speak. He prayed that Jimmy would keep his eyes shut, so he wouldn't be fixed in their piercing blue gaze; wished that the man would ease himself away, even by an inch or two. They were too close together, although Jonty couldn't increase the distance himself. Not now.

Jimmy turned, giving his friend the full force of his intense gaze. "You've not answered my question."

I can't trust myself to. Orlando would have been able to put some explanation to this—the magnet working on an iron filing or the call of the native river for the salmon. Jonty was afraid even to try to define what was going on. He was scared that he knew all too well. He turned slowly, giving Jimmy as cold a stare as he could conjure up. "I'll go when I'm ready, not before or after."

Jimmy laughed. "That's your Orlando talking, there. He's certainly rubbed off on you, hasn't he?" He reached over with a quiet confidence and put his arm around Jonty's shoulder. "I hope it's all been for the better."

Jonty shivered. Jimmy's flesh felt so cool against his own fevered skin, so smooth and fascinating. This was unbearable. "Oh, it has." Jonty closed his eyes, taking a deep breath before opening them and looking around. "We need to talk. This is too public a place."

Jimmy developed what could only be described as an idiot grin. "That sounds the sort of thing I've been waiting a long time for you to say."

"Maybe you shouldn't get your hopes too high, just yet. I'm being serious."

"So am I." They clambered out of the water, making their way through the changing rooms to a small cubicle used primarily for taking one's rest in a warm, yet not too hot, atmosphere. "We can talk here, there's no one to overhear us." Jimmy leaned closer to his friend, the gap between them narrowing to barely an inch. "They couldn't hear anything we do now."

Jonty felt the rise and fall of Jimmy's chest, the ripples of excitement coursing through his own flesh. "I know." He leaned back against the wall, the cool tiles easing his sweating shoulders. "I know that very well."

Orlando had returned to their suite to read through the notes from Bredon's interview once more. The entire perspective on the case had changed and he was struggling to get a grasp on it. He'd have rather got a grasp on Jimmy's neck, but that was by-the-by. The effects of too much thinking, lots of worry and a large lunch had left him drowsy and he soon succumbed to the arms of Morpheus.

He rarely dreamed if napping during the day, but this time he was plagued by the strangest visions. First of all he, Jonty and Hair-oil Harding were wandering the streets of Bath looking for some missing clothes which were said to have belonged to Mrs. Stewart, or possibly Lavinia. Then they walked along the river, only to find themselves in London and in a different guise. Jonty had somehow become a not very convincing dark lady, Jimmy was the rival poet, and Orlando was the Bard. He punched the man's nose, of course, which was gratifying, after accusing him of getting Jonty pregnant and not even saying sorry.

At this point, with the wondrous illogicality that the dream world is built upon, Lady Macbeth strode into the room, looking for all the world like Mrs. Stewart, only twice as determined. She told Orlando that if he couldn't do the deed then she would. Orlando handed her the dagger he found at his side, only he wasn't entirely sure which deed was being referred to. Helena Macbeth then waltzed off, with the three men in pursuit and the lady shouting—in a voice both cloyingly feminine and utterly terrifying—things about avenging her house.

Orlando woke in a muck sweat and within five minutes knew who had committed the murder of Sarah Carter, although he wasn't entirely sure why. This was information that had to be shared and, aversion to the House of Sulis notwithstanding, he'd have to get down there and share it. He tidied himself up and sped off towards the river, excitement bubbling up as he strode along. He knew who'd done the murder and he'd be Jonty's hero again. Then they could both go crack open some champagne or go and be rude to Jimmy Harding; either would be fun.

The cold, nagging thought that Jonty mightn't be at the baths, that he could well be off somewhere with Jimmy, laughing and doing all the sorts of things *they* were supposed to do together, was ignored until he reached his destination.

"Nice to see you again, Dr. Coppersmith." Millar greeted him with a smile. "It's nice and quiet today."

"Dr. Stewart's here, I hope?"

"He is that, sir. Just him and Mr. Harding."

Some idiot had made the room spin on its head. They must have done, to make Orlando feel so sick.

"Are you all right, sir?"

"Yes, thank you, Mr. Millar. I just walked here a little too fast." *Not fast enough.* "I'll have a little sit down, before I..." He left the sentence unfinished, turning and walking with unseeing eyes to the changing room. He opened the door gingerly, afraid he'd catch Jonty and Smarmy Chops *tête-à-tête*; instead, he caught a glimpse of two retreating backs going into one of the little anterooms, Jimmy's arm lightly resting on Jonty's shoulder.

Suddenly he didn't give a damn who had killed Sarah Carter. The world had just ended.

Chapter Thirteen

The waters looked enticing, even more enticing than the ones at the House of Sulis. Orlando stared into their depths, wondering if he should just vault over the parapet of the bridge and have done with it. He was a good swimmer—would that make drowning easier or harder? Wouldn't it be easier to find a knife and do what his father had done?

The small still voice of sense in his brain kept telling him that he was overreacting, that he shouldn't jump to conclusions, the very thing he'd scoff at his students for doing. He should go back and ask Jonty what the hell was going on; there could be a simple explanation.

The louder voice, the one full of self-doubt, told him he'd be better off not knowing what went on in that small room. The world had ended and he might as well end with it.

📖

"You've got me alone." Jimmy leaned on the wall next to Jonty, the distance between them hardly a hand's breadth. "What now?"

Jonty's breath felt hot in his throat; when his voice eventually appeared it sounded huskier than he'd ever remembered it. "You asked me to say—to your face—that I'm not interested." Every word was an effort. "I'm stating that plainly now." He sighed in relief that he'd not actually said, "Please kiss me."

Jimmy may have looked disappointed, but Jonty knew he was a good actor. He'd seen plenty of evidence on that front. "Do you really mean it? That I've got no chance whatsoever of getting my heart's desire?"

"Oh come on, I'm hardly that."

"But you are. I mean it. That's why I've fought so hard, even though I know you love Orlando. It's what all men do, fight for the thing they value above all else." Jimmy moved closer to his quarry. "It's natural."

"And it strikes me the more I say no, the more you pursue me." Jonty faced his predator square on, clenching his fists so his fingers couldn't go wandering anywhere near Jimmy's magnificent chest.

"The thrill of the chase, Jonty. It makes everything all the more pleasurable when you succeed. But if the answer's no, it's no, and I'll accede to your wishes. Only—" Jimmy smiled and leaned his face towards the other man's, "—do I get just the one kiss, for friendship?" He closed his eyes, seeming full of confidence his request would be complied with.

Instead he got a hefty thump on his nose, exactly the sort of punch which Orlando had dreamed of delivering to the rival poet.

"Hell, what was that for?"

"For not giving up. For being too bloody attractive by half and making the last week a misery. You can thump me one in return if you want and we'll be quits, then we can produce that play of yours together on even terms." Jonty stuck his chin out, waited for the punch, but all Jimmy did was roar with laughter.

"And spoil your looks? Not on your life. At least I can look

185

at you and admire the view again. I couldn't do that if your nose was all skew-whiff." Jimmy felt his own handsome proboscis, reassuring himself it was just as cute as it had always been. He took up a towel and wiped away some drops of blood, while Jonty joined in the laughter.

"I always said I suspected that you enjoyed getting yourself thumped. Now I know it's a fact." Jonty's voice shook with relief. He'd passed the test, the one he'd half decided he'd never succeed at.

"It's the last time I let myself be tempted into small rooms by the half promise of delights to come." Jimmy grinned despite the blood.

Jonty suddenly felt himself transported back twenty-five years. Perhaps he had even unwittingly re-enacted the last few moments of Sarah Carter's life, luring a victim with false promises only to deliver the killer blow. He felt more than uncomfortable when he realised what might have gone on in this room had Jimmy been determined to have his way or if he'd had to defend himself to the bitter end. An outcome even worse than if he'd succumbed, if only marginally.

A single sentence stirred in his brain. *Fight for the thing they value above all else.* Someone had come and killed Sarah Carter because of something which they valued above all else, of that he was now certain. Something which they wanted and she'd deprived them of, or so they thought. And he knew what the thing was.

"What's up? You look as if you've had a revelation."

"I have. I think I know why a murder was committed here. And I hope that Orlando can supply the identity of who did it."

"Your Orlando, he's a lucky guy. Wins at everything in the end."

"You should tell him that." Jonty sighed and picked up his

towel. "Perhaps he'd believe it, then."

Jonty bounded through the door of the changing room like a great hound, straining at the leash to get back to his hotel.

"Ah, Dr. Stewart." Millar rose from his chair. "Did Dr. Coppersmith catch you?"

"Is he here? Have I missed him?"

"He went through to the changing rooms not ten minutes ago, sir."

A small voice piped up. "Excuse me, Mr. Millar, but if Dr. Coppersmith is the man in the charcoal grey suit, he came almost straight back out." The lad who kept the changing rooms tidy seemed delighted to be able to impart such momentous information. "And he went out the door looking like, well, looking like thunder if you'll excuse me, sir."

Bloody hell. It didn't need a genius to work out what had happened. "Thank you, gentlemen. I see I'll need to catch him up." Jonty stuck on his hat—any which way, illustrating how disturbed he was—and almost ran out the door.

📖

Orlando had left the bridge; he didn't dare stay after a passing policeman had started asking solicitous questions. There were still lights on up at the folly—he should climb up there, find out Jimmy's address, go and murder him and then throw himself in the river, when it was too dark for the policeman to see. At least then Jonty couldn't have the swine to comfort him once *he* was gone.

"Orlando."

He heard the voice behind him but ignored it. It couldn't

really be Jonty, not yet. He'd still be at the baths, frolicking with Smarmy Guts.

"Orlando."

His father had suffered these, at times of great stress. *Auditory hallucinations* the doctor had called them; *ignore it and it would pass* was his advice.

"Orlando bloody Coppersmith, I can't run any more, I've got a stitch. Would you please stop and let me talk to you." Jonty came gasping along the road, red faced and hair wet, his hat having been discarded and now being used as a fan. "What the hell is going on?"

"I might ask you the same thing. You and Jimmy bloody Harding at the House of Sulis." Orlando couldn't look his lover in the eye.

"Me and Jimmy? We were talking, that was all."

"Talking? That's an interesting euphemism. You were whispering in his mouth, I presume? And don't you dare laugh."

"I can't help it. Dear God, Orlando, you're magnificent." Jonty laid his hand on his lover's arm, let it be shaken off then laid it there again. "You've jumped to a conclusion, a reasonable one, but you didn't have all the evidence. Look at this."

"What happened to your hand?" Orlando held up his lover's fingers in the dwindling light, noticing the redness of the knuckles and the slight traces of blood on them.

"It's part of the evidence you missed. My fist and Jimmy Harding's nose had a bit of a coming together. He cornered me at the baths, made a pass at me, then I took umbrage and had to get him somewhere I could thump him without all the world seeing. Oy, not in public!"

Orlando released his lover from his sudden fierce embrace. "Good for you. I wish *I'd* done it, but good for you all the same."

He thought of the river, the bridge, his own idiocy. How the world had turned full circle and come back to life. "I'm so sorry. I've been such an idiot. I even thought about..." He couldn't even bear to admit what he'd been contemplating.

"Jumping off the bridge?"

"How did you know?"

"Because you're the thing I know and love best in all the world. You can't help what you are, Orlando—I never knew your father, but he comes out in you at times, I see that. It won't stop me loving you forever." Jonty's face lit up in one of his most beautiful smiles. "I wish you'd heard what Jimmy said, about you. 'Your Orlando, he's a lucky guy. Wins at everything in the end.'"

"He said that?"

"He did. And meant it." Jonty slipped his arm through his friend's. "Walk me home, please, and I'll tell you everything that happened at the House of Sulis and you can tell me everything that happened in your head."

The air grew humid as they walked back, a sultry night in prospect, but heat wave or hurricane wouldn't have mattered to them. Nothing would have penetrated the shell of love they'd constructed again between themselves and the world. The sight of the Grand reminded them of unfinished business.

"I know about the murder." They both spoke at exactly the same time. The almost telepathic link that was growing between them, that inclined them to knowing exactly what the other was thinking, had sprung back into operation, no longer clogged with thoughts of Jimmy Harding.

"You first." Orlando nodded enthusiastically.

Jonty's face seemed awash with light, like some Titian hero, superbly crafted. "I think I know why it was done. Not *who* yet, I was hoping you'd oblige with that."

189

"We'll have rationale first, please, then I can see if my guess about the culprit works. Only wait till we're back in our room so I have light to read by."

"It is a bit dark, isn't it? Wouldn't be surprised if there's a storm brewing." Jonty shivered.

When they'd reached their suite, Orlando sat down and opened his notebook, Jonty following suit.

"Right, key point one—the child. Either someone killed Sarah Carter because she'd refused to marry Jeremy Weir and was supposed to have got rid of his baby, the one the family desperately wanted, or she was murdered because she got rid of what someone else believed was his child. Not that I think there was a baby, any more than I think there was a husband, but the killer didn't know that." Jonty ticked the points off on his fingers. "I believe they lured her with the promise of a lovely new necklace, enticing her into that little room so they could present it to her without anyone else noticing. She was half dressed and carried the rest of her clothes with her. The killer recognised them as being incriminating, had possibly given them to her himself, and so took them. That's point two."

Orlando ignored the slight frisson at the thought of luring people into little rooms. "All this indicates Jeremy Weir, of course, killing her because she'd lied about not being able to marry him—perhaps he discovered she'd been giving him the runaround with her nonexistent sailor-boy spouse. That, on top of apparently getting rid of his child, could be enough to drive a desperate man to murder."

"It is, which brings me to what worries me—point three, the flowers. The only way I can rationalise it is if Jeremy's brother still supplies floral tributes from his estate."

Orlando looked at his notepad, a half-hidden, smug grin threatening to cover his face. "Jonty. I think you've got it—well, nearly got it. I have a name here which would fit in very well with your theory if we just took it and jiggled it around a bit. Want to guess who it is?"

"Not Appleby." Jonty spoke decisively. "I suspect if he'd been fired up for revenge over the baby, he'd have taken it hot, when he was told about the child. It must be...oh, Orlando. Orlando. However will I tell Mama?"

"Leave it until tomorrow. Everything will seem better then." Orlando laid down his notepad, putting aside the intellectual for the sensual. He rose, drawing Jonty up to stand with him and worming his arms around the man's waist. "I should have known he'd never be able to wheedle you away from me."

"Yes, well, I do wish you'd leave something for other people to try to wheedle away. If you hug me any closer I'll expire." Jonty grinned, wriggling himself out of the tight grip. "Can you hear that?" A fierce rumbling, out to the west over the Bristol Channel, made them turn to the windows to see jagged shafts of lightning piercing the murk. "I guess it means I'll 'go off', as usual. Why now?"

"It'll be fine. Whatever happens, I'm here." Orlando held Jonty closer again, kissing his hair, willing and praying that his lover's normal reaction to storms wouldn't happen.

"Why tonight of all nights? The very time I want to stay *here*."

"Then we'll wait to make love until later, or tomorrow. We've all the time we want now, haven't we?"

"I suppose so." Jonty sighed, resting his head on his lover's shoulder. "This seems all higgledy-piggledy. These conversations normally go the other way around, with me having to reassure you about something or other."

"Time the tables were turned, then." Orlando started to gently pull the shirt from the waistband of Jonty's trousers.

191

Easy did it. "Sauce for the goose and all that." *Keep him talking and laughing, keep him here.*

"I'll give you the goose, or *a* goose perhaps." Jonty grinned. "I do feel so much better than normal, you know. I always get some sort of forewarning of my impending 'journey'. Like Papa gets when he's got a migraine in the offing. But I don't feel it tonight, even though I can hear that bloody thunder getting closer. Ain't it odd?"

"It's nothing short of marvellous." Orlando's hands started their ascent of Jonty's spine. "I'm not sure if it's just me but suddenly I feel very cold. That fire's damped right down—shall I stoke it up? And what, prithee, is so very funny?"

"You. Come on, we can find better ways to warm ourselves."

There were no complaints from Jonty this time over how long it took to divest Orlando of his shirt, each button eased from its hole with languorous simplicity, interspersed with kisses and moans. There was no need to rush things, no thoughts of other men to be fought against, only the thunder still crashing about and even that wasn't having its usual effect.

One of the things Orlando liked about making love was the juxtaposition of novel and familiar. The comforting landmarks en route—the point at which his naked chest could lie pressed against his lover's, the moment when Jonty's hand first made contact *there*—interspersed with fresh delights. How could anyone get bored with such wonders? Why should men go seeking prostitutes when their own beds could be such gardens of delight?

"Why do they do it, Jonty?" Orlando's thoughts had slipped into words, without their begetter's permission.

"Why do who do what?" Jonty doodled on his lover's chest, used by now to Orlando's peculiar questions.

"Go to women like Sarah Carter? Why not stay in their own beds?" Orlando's hands began to doodle as well, making diagrams that were in no way mathematical but just as dear to him as any demonstration of Euclid, mainly because they were drafted out on his lover's skin.

"A hundred reasons, or maybe just one at heart. The search for something they don't possess. Thrills, lust, love—not all marriages are as happy as my parents', you know, nor every relationship as fulfilled as ours has been. Think of Ralph and Lavinia. Were my brother-in-law not as noble as he is, he might have sought physical solace elsewhere."

Orlando thought again about the chance that Jonty would have sought physical solace elsewhere. His drafting took on a southerly direction, the diagrams becoming more artistic than geometrical, until they focussed around a particularly splendid part of Jonty's anatomy.

"Ah. That action, my love, is one of the reasons why I feel entirely happy to remain in the environs of this bed. Or the one at Forsythia Cottage. Or any couch in which you reside. Especially when you move your hand there. Oh." Jonty gasped, as he always did when Orlando began his tender assault of the key area of engagement. "Your hands remind me of an old-fashioned line of ships, setting up a blockade, sailing back and forth until they're ready to go in and make a raid. Just like, ah, that." Jonty's breath came shorter now. "I think I'll surrender all my fleet to you. Take it and use it as you will."

"You do have the most incredible imagination." Orlando let his assault ships run riot among the enemy's vessels, stirring up the great guns.

"But of course." Jonty broke off to regain his breath. "This is stimulus for any man of spirit. And if I may carry on the analogy—" he moved his fingers purposefully across the plain of

Orlando's stomach, "—I have a siege to set here. Such a stunning castle to assault." His hands found their target. "Here's the great tower, and when you descend you find the courtyards."

Orlando wasn't sure if the keeper of the castle would be able to stand much more interest in either courtyards or tower; flesh and blood could only take so much.

"And then there's the dungeon." Jonty's voice was increasingly hoarse. "There's a prisoner here, standing to attention and ready to be marched into that dungeon should it be required of him."

"You do talk twaddle." Orlando could barely speak now. "When we first met I used to long to go walking with you, to listen to you waxing lyrical about the river or the flowers. Now it's prisoners and dungeons, for goodness sake." He wrapped his legs around Jonty's thighs, pulled him close. "If you want to...to penetrate me...I'm prepared."

"Are you absolutely sure? It's a big step." Jonty's eager body gave the lie to his words. The prisoner wasn't just geared up, he was straining at his leash. "I really can't believe I'm hearing this. Not the Dr. Coppersmith of the 'dirty books' episode speaking, surely?"

Dr. Coppersmith of the dirty books hadn't had the threat of a rival to act as extra incentive to venture into strange waters. "What's the worst that could happen? If I don't enjoy it we don't have to be so bold in future." Orlando was feeling exceptionally audacious, intoxicated with the warm evening, the close proximity of an exquisitely masculine body and the thought that Jonty still hadn't 'gone elsewhere' even though the storm was at its height.

Jonty ran his fingers back to the dungeon. "If you're serious, it would make me happy beyond all measure. Even if it's just this once."

"I can think of nothing better than to make you happy. And I know I'm safe with you, safer than I've been with anyone else in all my life." Orlando began to tremble, a potent mixture of excitement and apprehension working on his nerves. He gently caressed the small of his lover's back.

"I'll be so gentle, so tender. You'll hardly feel a thing."

"Jonty, you complete idiot, there's not much point if I'm not going to feel a thing, is there?"

Jonty didn't reply with anything more than a giggle. He began, slowly, carefully, to take Orlando through the procedure, as caringly as if his lover were made of crystal. When union was achieved, a slow, calm amalgamation, Orlando could have sworn he could take no more—not because of distress but the sheer astonishing bliss of the moment. He'd expected something a bit uncomfortable, something he'd have to get used to, yet it had been wonderful.

"Jonty." His voice sounded small, tentative in the darkness, the stillness broken only by his lover's slowing breaths. "Still here?"

"Still here. Always will be."

The world had turned again and the last part of his happiness had fallen into place. For the first time since they'd met, the first time since he'd been a boy, Jonty hadn't "gone away" when the storm came. Galatea had turned out to be an Aesculapius too.

📖

"After all these years, you've come to me." The duchess looked calm and composed, much more so than her inquisitors felt. Her pleasant house, beautifully laid out and aglow with sunlight, felt oppressive to them. More like morgue than morning room. "I shall not deny it, there's no point. I think I have been waiting for this day."

"Someone in this case has already said that the mills of God grind slow. Perhaps you've been expecting them to get round to you." Jonty smiled kindly. Now they'd worked it out and come up with what they believed was the motive for the crime, he wasn't unsympathetic to the murderer. A life had been taken, nothing could justify that, but at least he could understand the motivation.

"Indeed. I've been making what small amends I could these last twenty-five years. Flowers on a grave may not seem very much, but at least they show that the girl is remembered and that I wish to acknowledge my mistake."

"About the child? The heir which might have been born illegitimate and therefore unwanted?" Jonty's voice was quiet and constrained.

"Dr. Stewart, do you think that, given our family circumstances, any of us would have sought to do away with the chance of an heir, whichever side of the blanket it would have been born? We'd have fought tooth and nail to legitimize the child somehow, to prove without doubt it was a Weir." A guarded silence fell on the room.

"The child never was Jeremy's, was it? It might well have been Appleby's—did you find that out very soon after Sarah Carter was killed?" Orlando's voice sounded kind, more kindly than it might have been to Critchley or Bredon.

"Something Thomas Critchley said at Lady Logan's a few months after the funeral made me wonder. I contacted Brian Appleby, who told me that the baby had been his. He'd asked the girl to be rid of it and she, he believed, had obliged, although she said that it had been miscarried. She had a habit of lying, you know."

Jonty sighed. "I know. For so long when investigating this case I felt desperately sorry for Sarah Carter, the girl whom everyone spoke so well of, who was such good company. And now we find that she was..." He shrugged.

"She was a manipulative little minx, Dr. Stewart. She told Jeremy that she couldn't marry him because she already had a husband and then it turned out she was just deliberately misleading him."

"Who told you that, Your Grace?" Orlando leaned forwards, confidentially, his detective skills much more developed than they'd been even a year previously.

"*She* did, when we spoke in that little room. At the place where all the debauchery went on."

"How long had you known that Jeremy was meeting her at the baths?"

"Almost from the start. I'd been suspicious—he never could lie to me with any success—and so I followed him one night and watched the comings and goings. At first I thought that the one they called Clarissa was 'her' but she soon put me right."

"You spoke to Clarissa?"

"Dr. Stewart, you do ask the most ludicrous questions. Of course I did. When she gave me the dates and times of their next gathering, putting the plan into action proved simple." A strange look of pride lit the duchess's face. "When I asked Sarah Carter why she had refused my son, she laughed in my face and said she had better fish to fry. 'And if he wants to know about my husband,' she gloated, 'then you can tell Jeremy he's all my eye and Betty Martin.' I was infuriated."

"How did you entice her into such a small room? Wasn't she suspicious?"

"It was easy." The duchess tossed her head scornfully, as if speaking of a maid dismissed for dishonesty. "Just the promise of a string of black pearls to go with the outfit she had been wearing. Actually they were haematite but she wouldn't have been able to spot the difference. I showed her them then told her I didn't wish to be seen giving them to her, for the family's honour and so forth. She trusted me implicitly—probably thought she'd been given a reward for services rendered to Jeremy—so she picked up her clothes and came."

"You took the clothes afterwards so that they couldn't be recognised and risk the family name being linked to the girl? Did you use the beads to strangle her?" Jonty felt like he was completing a jigsaw puzzle and the missing parts were essential to see the whole.

"The very same. You'll think that I'm callous, but I truly believed she had, quite heartlessly, destroyed the chance of our family line continuing."

"There's one thing puzzles me. How did you come to find out about the baby?" Orlando was tapping his notebook, another element to the detective persona he'd adopted.

"Critchley, again. He'd found out, but only got half the story, as usual. He assumed the child was Jeremy's and was *with child* himself to tell me. He's a nasty little man—your mother never liked him."

"And what puzzles me—" Jonty felt like he and Orlando were beginning to resemble Tweedledum and Tweedledee, "—is how you could have assumed at that point that there wouldn't be an heir in the family. What about Gerald, newly married? Or Jeremy himself, still in his prime?"

"Fecundity does not run in our family, Dr. Stewart. Despite my hopes for my youngest son." The duchess smiled in obviously fond remembrance. "And I knew my eldest couldn't oblige. He'd been ill in his youth and the doctors were sure that he could never sire a child. Can you imagine how mad I was when I heard that a potential heir had been done away with? I made my plans to go down to the House of Sulis and simply walked through into the changing rooms. I had no trouble finding Sarah Carter's booth, from the fact that it was my old dress lying discarded there. I suppose I was lucky not to be spotted, although I've always found that boldness pays off, something your mother would support. I even knew the layout of the building from when it had been respectable and they had open evenings where the quality was allowed to view the facilities."

Orlando noted all this in his book, shaking his head. "So you planned to kill her? It wasn't some spur of the moment thing when you learned of her lies?"

The duchess shrugged, surprisingly gracefully. "I don't know. I wanted to be told the truth, but I never got to hear about the true fate of the child. When I heard that she had lied to my son, spurning him in such a shameful way, I took that necklace of beads, it had a good heavy string, and simply drew them tight around her neck. She didn't have time to call out, I saw to that."

"So—" Jonty spoke quietly; he knew that this was going to be desperately difficult. They'd passed the point of no return—this would all have to be reported to the authorities—but he didn't know how the duchess would react to the last revelation they had to make. "So you never found out that the baby was as fictitious as the husband?"

Her Grace turned deathly white. "Never. That can't be true."

"It's what the person who knew Sarah Carter best alleged. It had been another story, told to Brian Appleby to goad him into offering to marry her. The strategy didn't work." Jonty studied his shoes; he truly dreaded having to tell his mother what had transpired. "And it led to her death."

The duchess didn't speak for several minutes—none of them did. All that broke the silence was the ticking of the clock and the sounds of the birds in the trees.

Eventually she simply stood up, moved to the window and said, "Call for the butler, please, and he can call for the police. Inspector Rumford is a good man—he was very helpful in the matter of my burglary and will be most discreet. I shall tell him everything." She turned, smiling graciously. "I would be grateful if you would be here to witness the proceedings."

📖

Two hours later, the two fellows of St. Bride's—much anguished and feeling as if they had been put through a mangle—emerged from the duchess's house in search of a cab and, ultimately, a bottle of claret. Or beer. Or anything which might revive them.

"She planned it all, I'm sure. An old friend of my mother and she turned out to be a cold-blooded murderess. I really thought it was a spur-of-the-moment thing, like old Mrs. Tattersall, but she had it all scoped out, Orlando, I've no doubt."

"The inspector says that she will probably be tried. She wants to be, I suspect. Wants it all to be out in the open. There's no family name to be ruined now—there's no family left after Gerald goes."

"I shall ring Mama as soon as I've had a glass of something. Need to get it over and done with." Jonty fiddled with his tie; it wasn't an interview he relished.

"Well, don't just rely on the Dutch courage. I'll stand and

hold your hand as you do it." Orlando patted his friend's shoulder.

Jonty smiled. "I'm bloody lucky to have you and I near as dammit made a complete hash of that with Jimmy. I'll never be so silly again."

📖

Three letters arrived at the Grand Hotel in between the solution of the mystery and the opening performance of *Macbeth*.

The one addressed to Orlando simply said, *At last I learned that you can't always get exactly what you want. You're a very lucky man, but I guess you always knew that. Harding.*

Jonty's was equally brief. *Sorry that our ambitions could not coincide. Really did hope that you'd be the one, at least for a while—didn't understand the depth of your devotion. He's very, very fortunate. Please still send a card at Christmas. You'll be a great tree. Break a leg, as they say.*

The third was addressed to them both and was technically a telegram, but one of great length. *You are both very sensible and brave boys who know how to do your duty without letting emotions get in the way. For all that it pained me to hear about Lavinia...*

"Dear Lord, Orlando—that's who my sister was named after. Extraordinary."

...you were quite right to see justice served. People must face up to what they have done. I can't say I'm not sympathetic towards what she did; family means an awful lot, my dears, so I will see that she is well supported if that son of hers doesn't come up trumps. I doubt she will hang at such a remove; Richard is off to see what can be done although it will no doubt be a

mess. But it was still the right thing to do. I'm proud of you.

📖

The opening night of *Macbeth* proved to be a success beyond everyone's expectations. Jimmy Harding, nose sufficiently recovered from its encounter with Jonty's fist to allow him to be a handsome and dashing Banquo, was glowing with pride as his company took the stage and received the absolutely warranted applause.

Orlando was there not just to support his lover—that had always been his intention—but to accompany Mrs. Stewart. The great lady had sent a telegram the day before to say that her husband had been asked at the last minute to escort the Duke of Connaught and she wasn't prepared to be sitting at home mumchance while the boys had fun. She'd arranged for herself and Orlando to have a pair of seats on the environs of the royal party.

It had become a sort of established fact among certain circles that Mrs. Stewart had a ward who was a very shy and extremely learned doctor of mathematics, who needed to be taken out and aired on occasions. If her husband was party to keeping up this slight deception, then he would wink at this slightest of white lies.

Orlando enjoyed the evening, especially treasuring the rather loud asides from the duke himself in the direction of Stewart senior. It took the royal personage two whole acts to realise that Lady Macbeth was being played by a man—an enormous shock for him, as he'd looked flirtatiously in her direction once or twice. During the interval he averred that "she" reminded him of young Helena Forster in her pomp, which caused the lady concerned to bristle somewhat, especially when Orlando was naughty enough to suggest that her son might have had a hand in fostering the likeness.

He knew he would pay for it good and proper when word got back, but he was beyond caring. Jonty was his, his alone, and he'd punched Jimmy on the nose for being persistent. It would have been better if it had been Orlando's own fist that had done the whacking but one couldn't have everything.

Jonty was a pretty convincing tree and led Birnham Wood down into Dunsinane, or at least round the corner of Ralph Allen's Sham Castle and across the stage a bit. The duke was impressed with this as well, muttering to Mr. Stewart at about one hundred decibels that he believed it the most convincing depiction of the scene he'd ever come across, most of the other representations he'd been forced to endure looking more like a party of boys with branches, out to play a trick on their sisters.

Jonty was, in Orlando's opinion, a lovely tree, a marvellous mountain ash or similar lithe and graceful plant, and he applauded wildly at the first possible juncture, reserving another tranche of appreciation for when they all took their bows at the end. He even kept back some applause for Jimmy who, he had to grudgingly admit, couldn't just act but spoke the lines perfectly in an authentic Scottish brogue.

Mrs. Stewart and her *young ward* joined the cast afterwards for a glass or two of champagne—not too much, as more performances were imminent over the next few days—and the lady seemed much impressed by Jimmy's charm and good looks.

As they made their way back to the hotel, she was both effusive and insistent that the charming man should come and stay in Sussex, making up the sort of stag party which had been so successful the Easter just gone. Orlando was noncommittal and diplomatic, leaving it to Jonty to suggest that perhaps that wasn't the wisest of ideas and if his mother wanted any more information on the subject, she should consult Miss Peters, who would give her chapter and verse.

📖

The train slowly pulled out of the station and the two fellows of St. Bride's snuggled into their first class carriage to admire the Somerset countryside for the short distance before it miraculously turned into Wiltshire. The large trunk with Orlando's name on it was safely stored in the luggage van alongside a case crammed full of books to grace the libraries of the university—and one or two which would be sneaked into Orlando's study. Jonty bore his pride and joy with him in a large brown briefcase: a finished manuscript, almost entirely typed up, of a book that would surely become a key reference work in the study of the sonnets.

They were looking forward to returning to Cambridge—albeit for only a few weeks before their real holiday began—not just for Mrs. Ward's excellent cooking but for a rest from the excitement of the past fortnight. Orlando had wished for another case and he'd got it in spades, more exhilaration and tension than he really knew what to do with. Jonty had wanted to understand jealousy and had experienced it from the inside, becoming his own dark lady. They would both be careful in future about what they actually wished for. Jimmy had been left behind both literally—he had a successful season of open-air theatre to preside over—and figuratively, Jonty having turned his back on any and all temptation. A salutary lesson, he felt, but one that he might have had to learn at some point.

The South of France was going to be beckoning soon. His mind, like his lover's, was already turning to university and domestic matters as they left the city of Aquae Sulis behind.

"You said that this was going to be a marvellous break. Still feel that in hindsight?" Jonty knew that the question was a dangerous one.

Orlando considered, sighed, then at long last nodded. "Aye. It may have been a bit more exciting than I was banking on but it's been wonderful in the end." He turned to Jonty and lightly touched his arm; although they were alone in the carriage they would take no chances. "I felt like we were passing through the fire at times. I spent so long wondering if Jimmy Harding was going to make good his threat, and if I'd known he was going to corner you at the baths, I would have..."

"Have what, Orlando? Thrashed him? I suspect he would have liked that, it would have made him even more determined." Jonty decided the time for candour had come. "It wasn't just at the baths, you know—he'd been making overtures before then. Several of them, that's why I got so upset."

"Then why didn't you tell me?" Orlando rolled his eyes, looking awfully like Lady Macbeth in one of his/her more dramatic moments.

"Because you would have gone mad. I had to deal with it all myself, overcoming him. I felt a bit like I was facing Rhodes and his minions once more—I didn't want anyone else coming in and rescuing me. I had to face my demons myself." If he was being slightly evasive about the truth of what those demons were, so be it for now; perhaps when they were both old and grey he might tell Orlando of how he had been tempted. But not yet.

"Do you think we'll ever see him again?"

"Who knows? I'll still send him a card at Christmas, that's simply being polite. Whether our paths cross again..." Jonty shrugged. He felt confident that if they did meet, he would be in control of the situation, but he wasn't going to tempt fate. He suddenly tapped Orlando's knee. "Come on, we have a lot of planning to do. You promised, absolutely swore, I remember, that once we were back from Bath, we could get this holiday organised. Mama has provisionally booked us some hotels and the old wagon lit but we do need to get a move on about making those into firm arrangements." He stopped, frowning. "You pouted."

"I did not."

"Oh yes, you did. I've not seen that expression for a while and when it occurs it's such a treat that I make a note of it. You pouted at the point when I alluded to France."

"Wouldn't you prefer the Isle of Wight? I hear that Ventnor is very like the Riviera and—" Orlando could continue no further. A hand had been placed over his mouth and a grinning imp was at the other end of it.

"France it is, Dr. Coppersmith, and you'll love every moment of it. I promise we shall go nowhere that smacks of Oscar Wilde, if that's your concern, and I shall not inflict escargots upon you. But you'd better get Mrs. Ward to air your bathers—we're for the Med!"

Epilogue

Dear Mama,

We have arrived all in one piece, connections completed and directions followed.

Orlando did not disgrace himself on the ferry this time—I rather think he might almost have enjoyed himself.

The hotel is marvellous and our suite has a lovely view of the Louvre.

I have plans to whisk "himself" past the restaurant tonight and find some café where we could share something exciting like a fondue. I live in hope.

Much love,

Jonty

Dear Mrs. Stewart,

I write this from the excellent hotel which you recommended. I am very grateful for your advice.

You will be pleased to know that the ferry crossing passed quite satisfactorily. I might even have enjoyed it if a certain person had not asked me every three and a half minutes whether I felt quite comfortable.

The menu for tonight looks most promising, although that said person keeps muttering about finding a café and eating bits of bread dipped in hot cheese. I will keep you informed as to whether I manage to avoid it.

Your friend,

Orlando Coppersmith

Dear Miss Peters,

Dr. Coppersmith and I are suffering a surfeit at present—not, you'll be pleased to know, of lampreys, but of historic buildings, gardens and antiquities.

You were quite right about the Mona Lisa; that lady has such a knowing expression on her face. I felt as if she were boring into my mind and examining my every thought. (Very vexatious when one had been recently studying the statues of Greek and Roman heroes.)

Dr. C. has a theory about the Venus de Milo which I dare not write on a post card.

I hope the rest of our holiday is as first class as the last few days have been.

Fond regards,

Jonty Stewart

Miss Peters,

You requested that I should write to you with my impressions of my first sojourn abroad. I am delighted to inform you that it is very agreeable. Paris is not a patch on Cambridge, but the city has its own charms.

I would say my only regret is that the ladies and gentlemen depicted in the Louvre had not been more modest in their choice of apparel. There is only so much voluptuousness one can take.

Please notify your brother that I have purchased the things he required, although Dr. Stewart says they will raise a few eyebrows as we come through customs.

Sincerely,

Dr. Coppersmith

Dear Mrs. Ward,

As I write this we are settling into our berths, having elected to take the overnight train; we do so want to see the sunrise over the Riviera.

You will be very pleased to know that the hotels and restaurants have all been very clean, although I suppose that bread, cheese, olives and white wine does not constitute your idea of a proper lunch.

We have been able to find laundry facilities which I hope will live up to the standards you require; if not I apologise in advance.

I shall seek for the very best tortoiseshell comb I can find, although I wish you had taken up my offer of bringing you back a Parisian hat.

Regards,

Dr. Stewart

Mrs. Ward,

I know you were very concerned about us eating nothing but snails and frogs' legs and all of them smothered in garlic, but the food has actually been quite acceptable. Even if Dr. Stewart has managed to smear bread and cheese all over himself on regular occasions.

We are settling into our wagon lit and will soon be speeding through the countryside, much of which we will not see until morning. Dr. Stewart assures me the South of France is a lovely place and Monte Carlo will be a treat. We shall see.

Sincerely,

Dr. Coppersmith

Papa,

You were entirely right in saying that I'd enjoy the Riviera much more with a friend at my side. Orlando has taken to life here absolutely like a duck to water. You should see him at the pavement cafés in his white linen suit, turning all the ladies' heads.

The train journey was truly excellent and the sun coming up over the cliffs was a sight to behold.

I shall endeavour to bring home as much of the wine you recommended as the customs men will let me; our portion we will simply have to drink here, alas.

We made a foray to the casino last night—while I remain a poorer but wiser Jonathan, Orlando is rolling in it.

Love,

Jonty

✉

Mr. Stewart,

I now understand why you praised France so highly. I am not ready to admit this entirely to your youngest son, but this has been an excellent holiday and all the things I viewed with trepidation have proved to be not daunting at all.

I would like to tell you about a little plan I put into operation at the casino. Dr. Panesar and I had devised a strategy, back at St. Bride's, that we were sure would yield fruit at the tables. It has proved entirely successful and reaped very handsome dividends. Jonty naturally says that it's "beginner's luck" and I will "come a cropper" and other coarse expressions, but I believe that the logical application of mathematics has been practically proven again.

Your friend,

Orlando Coppersmith

Maurice,

I do hope this card reaches you before Dr. Coppersmith's, as I wish you to be in possession of all the facts rather than just his no-doubt economical version of the truth.

He had been doing very well at the casino with the system you two devised, making steady but not suspiciously spectacular profits, but last night it went all ends-up and his faith in probability has been badly shaken. All his ill-gotten gains have returned to their natural home and he is rather rueful.

Otherwise all is very well—we live like lords and are gaining a taste for squid and other such outlandish delights.

Please give my regards to Nurse Hatfield should you see her.

Jonty

Dr. Panesar,

I have to report that my initial optimism regarding our scheme to take on the bank at Monte Carlo has received a severe denting. I believe the fault must lie in one of our original premises; I have made a record of all the results and hope we can go through them together to refine the scheme.

Dr Stewart has sneered at it all, of course, stating that it was simply beginner's luck followed by the natural workings of the law of averages—combined with a regression towards the mean and the homing instinct of the chips for the casino's safe.

Apart from this we are having an excellent holiday and the Mediterranean waters are warm and clear.

Should you happen to come across Nurse Hatfield, please convey my best wishes to her.

Dr. Coppersmith

Dearest Mama,

It hardly seems possible that tomorrow we will be packing our bags and beginning the trip home. It has been such a wonderful holiday and, if nothing else, it has been worth it to see Orlando's delight at eating a picnic on a secluded beach with the Mediterranean lapping at our toes.

I wonder if I will be able to persuade him to travel even further abroad next summer? As for this year, the only tangible evidence of our sojourn abroad will be Papa's wine, Orlando's tan and a bonceful of happy memories.

All my love,

Jonty

Dear Mrs. Stewart,

I have just time to send one last card before we catch the train. Your son suggested I keep it and post the thing when we reached home, a notion that seems scandalous to me.

I promised I would answer your questions at this point and the reply is yes, it has been absolutely wonderful but no, I do not wish I had done it years ago. It would have not been in the least bit pleasurable without a constant and true travelling companion at my side to savour the delights with me.

I hope we will get the chance to see you as we pass through London as I have some things to leave with you.

Your friend,

Orlando Coppersmith

About the Author

Charlie Cochrane's ideal day would be a morning walking along a beach, an afternoon spent watching rugby, and a church service in the evening, with her husband and daughters tagging along, naturally. She loves reading, theatre, good food and watching sport, especially rugby. She started writing relatively late in life but draws on all the experiences she's hoarded up to try to give a depth and richness to her stories.

To learn more about Charlie Cochrane, please visit her website www.charliecochrane.co.uk. You can send an email to Charlie at cochrane.charlie2@googlemail.com or join in the fun with other readers and writers of gay historical romance at http://groups.yahoo.com/group/SpeakItsName.

One hot night, one freeze frame…and one shocking surprise.

Tabloid Star
© *2009 T.A. Chase*

As a bartender at the Lucky Seven club, Josh Bauer could take a different guy home every night…if he wanted to. Working three jobs, however, makes it hard to connect with anyone. One man, though, is too much temptation to resist. A steamy encounter in a back alley leads to an explosive night of sex in Josh's bed—a bed he isn't surprised to find empty the next morning.

What does surprise him, though, is the front page of a tabloid. Apparently his one-night stand isn't as anonymous as he thought it was.

Ryan Kellar's career is taking off. Advance buzz about his movie says it's a blockbuster, and going home with the gorgeous bartender is the perfect way to celebrate. And he thought he'd gotten away clean—until the picture in the paper shocks him into reality. Was Josh really just playing…or playing him for a fool?

Trust isn't big on their list right now, but as their worlds fall apart, it's all they have. At least until they figure out who took the picture. And why…

Warning: Hot manlove, gratuitous licking of tattoos and dealing with stalking paparazzi.

Available now in ebook and print from Samhain Publishing.